THE
LEACHING

THE LEACHING

TYLER SIZELOVE

THE LEACHING

iUniverse books may be ordered through booksellers or by contacting:

iUniverse
1663 Liberty Drive
Bloomington, IN 47403
www.iuniverse.com
1-800-Authors (1-800-288-4677)

ISBN: 978-1-5320-3871-6 (sc)
ISBN: 978-1-5320-3872-3 (e)

Library of Congress Control Number: 2017918511

Print information available on the last page.

iUniverse rev. date: 12/12/2017

1

t was over as fast as it had started. The king's conflict would see another ninety-nine years of blood and chaos, but it was all over for the stubborn knight. How stupid he was—and how young. Sir Ramsey of the Warwick court was twenty-six years of age when he fought his first true battle, and most likely it would be his last, depending on how the king felt. He never thought he would cower so easily, but it took only some three hundred arrows in the first volley, cascading down like a maddening swarm, each arrowhead pelting the flesh of his men before him and killing them before they could fall.

Damn, Ramsey thought. *Who is this damnable man!* Ramsey was such a coward he'd even run from his remaining men who were without horses, stumbling in the hedges of the rugged French countryside. He still had ten of his best mounted fighters at his side, but even they were fifty yards behind. Perhaps it was not just the battle in front of that castle that scared him. Perhaps it was the castle. The heavy gallop of each stride the palfrey took was another pounding in his head. *The castle, the skins. Who is this man?* The image of the first wave of men captured deep in those woods had scarred him. Was war always this barbaric?

I have an army—well, not my army; my king's army—to protect me. I will not go back there. The grass was moist, unmolested by horse or wagons. Another mile, and the greenery was replaced by mud and tamped earth for easy travel. He passed local cottages, thatched houses, and farms until he placed his eyes upon true magnificence—King Edward's men at arms. Caen looked bleak under the new English rule, but Ramsey never thought it would be so beautiful. It was away from *there*. He reined in his tired horse, which had begun to buckle from the fatigue. Clumsily, he fell off, crashing into the mud. The two guards outside the largest tent in the outer encampment helped him up.

Sir Ramsey's eyes were half-closed at first and then wide open and shifting back and forth, as if he saw he was in the wrong place. The spearmen to his left wore slight grins. The spearmen pondered why this once clean, dark-haired, confident knight was now covered in dirt, blood, and what looked to be black soot, possibly from flame arrows.

"You look distraught, sir. War getting to you already?" Whether the guard spoke in jest or meant to be humiliating didn't break Ramsey's spirit; his spirit was already broken. His pride turned to fear as his life flashed before him. He regained his stance and motioned to his men, who now were dragging their feet or fumbling to down some water from the nearest well.

"My men ..." He almost forgot how to talk.

The left guard raised his eyebrows into his half helmet,

trying to guess Ramsey's next words. "I would think he needs a word with you." The guard jerked his head in the direction of the tent flap.

Ramsey could feel eyes on him from everywhere in the camp and village—from the villagers especially, who looked more frightened than curious. They turned their heads away from the exhausted Englishman to quickly resume their daily duties. The knight entered the tent, only to see an angry bearded man, clad in fine colorful garb, staring at him with utmost intensity.

Edward the Third leaned over his map table with fists planted on the oak surface. His eyes angled down, beaming through the soul of Ramsey. "You ignorant worm! Just what the hell are your insidious motives to kick at my sides?"

The king's anger was not enough to move him. Ramsey looked straight in Edward's stony eyes. "They're all dead. Lord Mumford, Your Majesty —I ... didn't think—"

Edward slammed his fist on the table, toppling a stack of books. "You fail to think! Do you expect me to claim these lands with short of over three thousand men, or should I throw weapons in the hands of peasants to take Calais? If Mumford was here right now, he would wish he would have died. But since he was most fortunate, this all rests on your shoulders, Sir Ramsey. The next time I approve of a scouting, I expect to see the party back in my grasp, with all limbs still attached and hearts still beating. But you ..." The king took a breath, wagging his finger. He stepped around the table to approach the tainted soldier. "I will not expect any more scouting ventures from you, will I? And certainly not any from Mumford." His voice

grew calm, but a solid stench of fury still lingered. "Sit," he commanded.

Ramsey plopped down on a cask and slouched over. The feeling of failure was only a slight itch, as Ramsey was more relieved than anything. The knight stared at the burning candle on the table, losing his thoughts in the flame, recollecting the events.

The king paused and then lifted his tent flap to steal a gaze outside at his defenses. He took a moment to look at some of the scouting men under Mumford.

The king noticed one of the priests and another servant extracting an arrow from a wounded rider, not a crossbow bolt but a long fletched arrow. He resumed his focus on Ramsey again, after offering him a flagon of wine. It was easy to imagine why getting drunk was Ramsey's priority. Edward dismissed that and asked, "This fortification … you know where it is? You were there?"

For a moment Ramsey quivered and narrowed his eyes, but before he could lie, he realized it was the *king* who had asked him a question. He nodded in response and then downed another gulp of red wine to shake off the anxiety.

Edward took up a chair across from him. "The ruling figure over the land—who is he?"

Somehow the wine was not acting quickly enough for the knight. The fire bolts from the scorpions, the deadly accuracy of the volleys, the flayed skins of those captured in the woods the day before—all this repeated in his thoughts. They had impaled the pink corpses on the perimeter stakes around the walls and dangled the hides over the parapets.

Edward spoke again, agitated. "You are to report everything you saw. That is your duty. Now ... did you get a name, see him, his banner, anything?"

Ramsey peered up to meet the king's eyes. "No," he murmured. The cavalry crashing in behind their rear rank replayed in his head. Ramsey suddenly got a bad headache, and the alcohol wasn't helping. Mumford had shifted his horse around to be met by a knight's lance in his throat. The fat lord fell from his saddle, clinging to the broken-off stump of wood lodged in his neck. Ramsey had withdrawn his sword and had lashed out at another closed-helm rider, but the foe's morning star had shot out before he could blink. The ball had missed the blade but the chain had wrapped around it. Ramsey's steel had been ripped from his hand, and the mounted knight had come back with a second ball that had landed on his right shoulder plate.

He could remember the spike of pain that nearly made him faint from the shock. The dent made the armor feel queer and tight around his arm. That's when it occurred to him that he was going to retreat. The horn had sounded before he could even give the order. The clanking swords and bunting shields had ceased as enemy cavalry had driven off the less disciplined.

The flame arrows were inhumane, as they also set men alight. He recalled their tunics and colors draped over the plate armor—a field of purple-and-red-striped chevrons with a black sun in the center. The elaborate design almost looked tribal with the flailing rays and sophisticated pattern. He relayed that much to the king.

Edward digested that information and collected his

thoughts. "A lording native to be sure, or even a relative to a noble to have that much power and men. Who is this man?" The question was not to Ramsey.

The battered knight took one last swallow of wine. Excess ran off his cheeks clumsily as he leaned forward. "He's no man."

* * *

Mont Saint Michel, present-day France

All her years of college had not prepared her for this. Her job as a historical analyst required more than just patience; it required a devotion to dig up as much as she could. Detail was everything. Her digging had lasted two hours in the historic library. The librarian was able to help her track down a few books, nearly the size of old VCRs, within the lavish wooden halls of the archives— *The Hundred Years War, the French Domain,* and *Minor Lords.* Amanda Cohen was enjoying the bulk of it, but the small details she was looking for did not stand out. She flipped a glossy page and discovered another part that discussed the first mistake of the English invasion. As successful as it was, this was not something every high school student learned. It was only less than a penny out of that entire campaign. Sir Ramsey Trembleton had somehow swayed the king to evade the southwest region altogether. France lacked unity, and other more important regions drew the king's attention. Château Noir Soleil, or Black Sun Castle, was far too sophisticated. Amanda almost could not believe it. After another scouting party was sent out with paramount caution, the reports further had proved that Edward should steer clear. He'd focused his conflicts north, along the coast.

Amanda looked again at some of the medieval art and oil paintings of two clashing armies. The images were cluttered with men in bright tunics holding banners, swords, and spears and wrestling in the center to gain control. No other information was provided about the castle. Amanda sat poised in her chair, twirling her fingers through her long black hair. Amanda was thirty-two years old, petite, with fair white skin and steady eyes. Most of her associates could not keep up with her, as Amanda was always on the move from one location to another, finding new clues and bits of information. The locals near the Black Sun site were quite familiar with the charismatic black-haired woman.

"Where are you?" she said to herself. She closed that book and had the library's assistant put the first two away. She rented out the third, *Minor Lords*. The senior librarian argued with her about walking out with that one, but once Amanda showed her a government research permit, there was no further discussion. She decided to get some fresh air and stop by a café overlooking the English Channel and the famous Saint Michel's castle, towering high up on the spit of land. Tourists were everywhere at this time of year. She slung the fifteen-pound backpack from her shoulder, with the book stuffed inside, hung it off the back of the chair, and ordered a cup of espresso. She watched as little mopeds and coupes buzzed by on the cobbled streets. *So many people,* she thought. She missed being out in the countryside again, with the quiet, peaceful sensation of the wind blowing and birds chirping. This new project, however, based out of the ancient Château Noir Soleil, was slightly eerie. There was almost nothing outside of those dark walls. No bird chirps, animals, or even wind rustling the leaves. As interesting as it was, she felt like she was being watched. The call back to the town for further research relieved her in that sense.

In her deep brooding, she was startled by another voice that called out, "Hey!" She quickly turned to see her coworker. Jean Keller was still in school but was engaged in the project with Amanda as an apprentice. Jean seemed happy to see her .

"Hey, you. Looks like your just as anxious as I am to get out," said Amanda, receiving Jean's hug.

Jean sat down and ordered a coffee upon the waitress's arrival. "Well, I'm not as traditional as you. I looked through some of the so-called scholarly sites and found nada. You?"

Amanda shrugged with a half-smile. "Not really much more than you. I managed to get out of there with one more reliable piece. The lady at the desk was about to breathe fire at me until she saw my permit. Working for LPS has its perks. I think this is going to be a long night for me." She looked at Jean, grinning at the young enthusiastic student. "So how are you enjoying it here? Anything interesting, other than thousands of dry articles on one region?"

Jean shook her head with a chuckle. "Well, I still feel so lost, almost frightened to just get out and explore. That and all these tourists …"

"Are scary? Yeah, I believe it, but that's why we have

a job—to educate. I was surprised at the last entry exam results."

"Exam?" said Jean.

"Yeah, the one for the seasonal grads who majored in French history. Probably have to blame the schools. Half of them presume the dukes of the Normandy were great men and leaders, when in truth they were greedy as hell. You'll learn more, working in my area; don't worry. Let's not delve too far into the negatives of the history, though. We are trying to tackle common environmental issues that the royal families and low-born faced day to day. The exhibits need to convey how they overcame these obstacles using medieval technology or even just ways of thinking. Religion mostly," explained Amanda.

Jean grinned in agreement. "Not everyone is as clever as you or as experienced, for that matter. And speaking of religion, I think I have something that might interest you."

Amanda squinted at her with her mischievous brown eyes. "So you *did* find something?"

Jean withdrew a CD from her handbag and gave it to Amanda. It was unmarked but Amanda stashed it in her backpack anyway. "Another university student from Paris loaned it to me. It may or may not help you, but I thought, eh, what heck? So first record dates back the 1300s?"

"Not exactly sure when the place was built, but it definitely was discovered by two of the king's loyal men, until they decided to go looking for plots of land to call their own when the war ended. If it was scouting that Mumford was up to, they may have lived. I'm also confused about something else."

Jean tilted her head. "What's that?"

"The arrows Sir Ramsey Trembleton described were long range, nearly three-foot shafts with finely crafted fletchers on the ends. Mumford's men were ambushed in the woods with those same powerful weapons. At this time, the English were the only ones with the new long bow capable of punching through armor. The French armies had archers but none as lethal as the ones portrayed at the battle of Black Sun. Even at Crécy, the French feudal knights were slaughtered by English long bows. It was a pure surprise, but this just doesn't seem right."

Jean nodded and thought for a second. "Maybe they had spies in England," she suggested. There was a possibility there, but the English had spent years beforehand perfecting their weaponry. The French also had little reason to believe England would invade, with even less reason to think that such technology could be improved to maximum killing potential. Amanda finished her drink in silence before making her leave.

"I'll see ya later," said Jean.

"Sure thing. Thanks for the info."

Don Millar was another of the few Americans amid the French and British crowd gathered in the orientation hall. Don was in his early forties and had a mess of short black hair. He had a slim jaw and round tired eyes and a face that conveyed skepticism. He always had a hint when something was amiss or even smelled straight bullshit. Perhaps that's why he was a security guard—really more like the head of LPS security. Most people would mistake Donald for a detective due to his sense of awareness and sometimes-peevish attitude.

He chose not to sit but to wait in the back near the entrance, leaning a shoulder on the nearest support column. The announcer up front was Phil Orrelle, a French regional relations coordinator for the project. He looked the part, with a groomed head of wavy hair, round spectacles, and a casual V-sweater and tie. Don always tried to read people and how they carried themselves. Don also liked having a gun on him and could not see how he would be caught without one. Looking at Phil, he knew that man never had worked hard a day in his easy life.

Phil had grown up in a family who were higher-up government bureaucrats—a rather fast way to become a leading member of a project that required all the historical knowledge of three different universities, journalists, authors, and countless other historians. Though Phil made some sense, he had a passion for history, just not a passion for grunt work.

Don had climbed the ranks of this world. A mechanic for a dad, who brought home just enough. A mother who tended a family of five and who also somehow managed to make and sell dresses for a small business in town. After Don graduated from school, he went into the police academy in a minor county in Ohio. That's where he took a liking to firearms and the basic order of things. Growing up in a house with four other screaming children had been enough chaos for Don, and he moved out as fast as he could. Eventually, the twenty-seven-year-old had gotten bored and looked up various international security firms all over the world. Travel was something he had always wanted, but he knew he would never get there if he was stuck in Ohio. Then he got the interview for the Landmark Preservation Society, which basically was an upscale organization that helped restore and open up medieval buildings, findings, and relics to the public. A location that attracted lots of people required lots of security, especially in the early stages of discovery, to protect from robbers and petty vandalism.

Phil was nearly done with the presentation. Don could only imagine how many of the city planners were dozing off.

"Now, the most important part here is delicacy. Time is essential, but we cannot rush recovery. Getting to the part with the tree line, as Mr. Dwaine mentioned earlier, we need professional arborists to bring down those rotting pines. The damage one of those trees can cause can set us back weeks or even months—" He was halted by a raised hand in the front row.

A chubby-cheeked reporter with a bow tie asked, "Sorry, but this is a castle made of stone that has sat for hundreds of years. I don't mean to disparage your inquiry, but how would a tree falling on the castle damage it?"

"Good question, but that is just it. It has been there many years and was exposed to winds, rain, snow, foundation erosion, and decay. A good amount of weight with a sudden impact could further tamper with the walls or even put a big crack in a few of the preexisting faults on the eastern side. Though most of the walls do look sturdy and remarkably intact, I cannot be too certain of its present condition."

Don felt a hand on the shoulder of his leather jacket. He turned and was greeted by the Landmark Preservation cofounder, another Brit, who had an honest smile, square

12

face with a dominating nose, and thin combed hair that was beginning to gray. His handshake was firm and strong.

"I always tell him to go easy, but he likes to talk about this bit of foundation like it was a movie trilogy," said Mark Timbaugh.

"At least the city officials won't have any doubts," added Don.

Mark's smile was one of satisfaction. He led them out through the exit doors into a long hall illuminated by fluorescent lights. Mark spoke as they walked. "Well, good news is we are nearly finished. Bad news is I won't need all of your mates when the castle is opened to the public. Any thoughts on who you might want to keep on your team?"

"Well, they have about another month on their contracts. Your people worked quicker than I thought. How much longer on the interior?" Don asked.

Mark pressed his lips together, resenting the request for an update. "At least two more weeks before it's ready. After that, the locals will hire their own guard crews."

Don took it well, but his expression implied he was upset. "Any other ruins you guys had in mind? Work is always needed, especially for some of these guys who have families. It's going to be hard to cut them short."

Mark nodded. "Totally agree, my friend. But I'm going to push Mr. Packard to send them compensation. We actually saved a lot, so your mates won't go home with less in their pockets. We have a temple in northeast India for which our coordinator is getting permission, but that's not for another year, at least."

The two men followed the hall into the main lobby of City Hall and stepped outside, getting a breath of fresh, cold air. Gray clouds gathered in the sky. The French locals kept to themselves, snuggled in their black coats and furry hats. The street performers were counting their coins and closing up their instrument cases.

After some thought, Don turned to Mark to shake his hand. "Compensation sounds like the best way to close this deal. I would hope to see you soon with the good news, or at least email me those figures," said Don, staying optimistic as much as possible.

"No worries, my friend. Until next time—and I've been meaning to ask, what are you going to do?"

"I'm going to do what I've always done after a project, Mark. Recruit people for the next one. You know I'm good until then," said Don, making his way toward the street.

"Take a load off. You're always trying too hard!" yelled Mark. He waved as Don chuckled and climbed into a little white cab.

2

Don stepped inside, away from the chill evening air. His hotel room lit up after the sensors picked up his body motion. It was a fancy hotel room that could be used for long stays. The entry hall flowed out into a small kitchen and dining room on the right, with a bedroom and bathroom on the left. He set the keys down on the counter with a jangle and withdrew a beer from the fridge. He enjoyed the luxuries of paid travel through the organization and decent hotel rooms, but none of it made him feel as whole as his family. His computer monitor lit up with the background wallpaper—a pretty woman with blonde frizzy hair and a six-year-old girl wrapped in her arms, both with big smiles.

Now forty-one years of age, Don found it harder to leave home on these long trips and working unknown lengths of time on a restoration project. This was his sixth one as a security employee. The police force was an ongoing subject replaying in his mind, and going back to settle down in Ohio was becoming more of a reality, especially if his wife, Sarah, got that dental career to help with bills and their second child, which was on the way.

It'd been seven months in France, which was faster than he expected. Usually the sites that were worked on or restored took over a year, but the budget system was well backed, now that Ted Packard and Mark Timbaugh had made reputable names for themselves. Countries as old as France and as well developed had been more than willing to pay for advanced technology that aided in the construction and marketing campaign. He took a swig of beer and noticed a live call coming in with the little funny *bleep–boop* sound echoing from his speakers.

He answered, and the same frizzy-haired beauty on his wallpaper showed on screen, only less vibrant and very groggy. She still managed a grin on her soft cheeks when she saw Don on camera.

"Well, look who's up," said Don.

"It's morning here, babe. Remember the time difference?" She chuckled at that.

"Ah, right. Still on the other side of the globe. Damn. But you know what?"

"Hmm?"

"Pretty soon I'll be wrapping it up here, and we'll be having some of that gourmet Chinese food from … that one place. What do you call it?"

She laughed again in the middle of her stretch. "You mean the Zhou Chow Grill, silly? Hmm, sounds nice, but I had shrimp on the mind."

Don faked a look of bafflement. "Zhou Chow ran out of shrimp? Impossible! Well, we better go to the other fake seafood place."

She laughed and turned to look at the little figure approaching the screen.

"Eww, shrimp!" The little girl seemed more energized and drawn to her dad's face.

"Don't be silly; you like shrimp," said Sarah. "And is that how you say hi to your dad?"

The girl wiggled around and came closer to the camera, making a straight grin with her little white teeth. "Hi, Dad! When you coming home?"

Don returned the grin. "In a few more weeks, hon. Don't you worry. And we don't have to eat shrimp—well, you don't, but I'm going to gorge."

"She's always changing her mind. When she sees you eat it, she will. Hey, Julia, go lie back down. You still have a while before school."

Julia said goodbye to her dad and headed back to bed, skipping down the hall.

Don was mesmerized by his wife's beauty, even if she wasn't wearing makeup.

"What you staring at, handsome?" she asked.

"Oh, you know, just the camera on my screen. Nothing much," Don teased.

Sarah laughed again and shook out her tangled hair. "How's it been over there? You buy any cool souvenirs?"

"Haven't been too much into the local life, but the job is good. Making whatever quick buck I can before these people replace us all with robots. Who really knows how long before the next project? The world is running out of old spooky places, I guess."

"Well, one day the little one and I want to see one of your 'spooky places'; sounds fun."

"Yeah, some of the ruins might be disappointing. Just some rocks in a field somewhere. This last one, though, was strange. I guess most of it is still intact."

Sarah looked surprised. "Really? Is that why you're coming back so quickly?"

"Suppose so. But I'd better update my log book and send some more messages. I will be back in no time," said Don. Sarah puckered her lips and blew out a kiss. "Okay, baby, love you," Don said and ended the call.

After breaking the news to his lower-ranking supervisors through emails, Don finished his beer and took a shower. His hotel room was silent some minutes later, all but the random footsteps in the room above him, which thrummed as he got in his bed and drew the covers over him. The light automatically shut off in the adjacent room. The humming of his computer still made a faint sound near the kitchen. Sleep mode was supposed to be on, and the unusual noise made him get up and check his screen. His pesky antivirus shield software polluted his display.

UNKNOWN USER ACCESS

He clicked on the *do not allow* option and shrugged off the possibility of anything genuinely suspicious. The firewall was still active. Before he could click to shut down his computer, it did so prematurely, with an unusual crash. The screen flickered to black, then white, and shut off. Now perturbed by the sense that he'd just been hacked, Don quickly pulled the plug on his router, killing the network connection instantly.

"Strange," he murmured. The screen was totally dark again, with no light showing from his monitor.

Click.

A noise from behind forced Don to turn around. The automatic light in the entry hall kicked on. Don didn't take any chances. He withdrew his compact pistol from his desk drawer and steadied it on the hall, but he could not see the door. It was this blind spot that made him question, if anyone were to enter, why they would stop in the entrance. As he panned to the right, however, there was no one there, just a locked door and a house plant. The light flickered off and then on again. An electrical surge? Ghosts?

He could think of only one thing that would affect both his computer and the lights—a static disturbance. A sort of electromagnetic pulse, or EMP, but who the hell would want to fire that up at ten o'clock at night? Don kept his pistol on his bedside table as he tried to forget it and go to sleep.

Morning peered through his blinds and brought Don out of bed. After getting ready for the day, he tried booting up his computer, and it started normally, with no trouble. The background sound of his coffeepot brewing was drowned out by a heavy knock on his door. Don checked the peephole and saw a heavyset man in his mid-thirties, looking around. Don opened the door and was greeted with a smile.

The man's English was slightly broken, as he refrained from his normal French. "Hi ... uh, mister ..."

Don nodded. "You can call me Don. What's up?"

The big man shifted. "Did you have trouble with your TV or lights last night? I was just wondering because my TV cut out. I wasn't ... uh ..." He started speaking in French, not knowing how to finish in English.

Don knew some of the language to help him out,

and he gestured toward his light. "*Oui*, computer crash and flickering lights. I'm guessing some sort of uh … *poussée*…perturbation. You know … in the power. It's not just your room," Don replied the best he could.

The neighbor strained a smile and thanked him after complaining about management.

Don finished making his coffee and was surprised by a phone call just as he slid on his jacket. He answered, "Millar here."

It was Phil Orrelle. "Bonjour, Monsieur Millar. I would like to thank you for your contribution to our project and for keeping our site safe. I have run the numbers with the local offices and treasurers to determine your bonus and, most importantly, compensation."

"Well, thank you, Mr. Orrelle, but Mark will be handling that with my team. I was unaware of any bonus, however. Would you care to elaborate on that?"

"Yes, absolutely. Would you have time for breakfast? I would much rather pick you up; no need for a cab."

Don's interest was piqued. He thought about the business he had with the recruitment agent, but realized it could wait until later. "Sure, ah … you know where I'm located?"

Phil confirmed the hotel's address and hung up. Don's payment usually came in through the LPS Finance Department, but this was different. Orrelle, being the coordinator, could have pulled some strings. Don waited by the front entrance of the hotel, under the red fabric canopy, pondering the new source of income for all his hard work. Or was it some sort of trick?

Amanda had so much more to do with the exhibit itself. Her research was coming to a close, but it was her junior historical assistant who found another piece of the puzzle and all of its little perks. The CD Jean had given her uncovered the truth—or part of the truth—behind the mysterious Hugues de Lamonthe. Amanda opened the blinds in her little apartment on the fourth floor. She enjoyed the sound and sight of rain tapping against her window while she did her research. The laptop screen was populated with a PowerPoint slide and paragraphs of written text of Lamonthe's biography. The medieval paintings of robed men and brutal battles sent shivers down her spine. Amanda was aware of this blood-soaked land she dwelt on—the untamed civilization of old Europe.

She was reminded of her first trip to Transylvania and Dracula's fortress on the high mountaintop. Looking down into the borderlands of the once-tainted soil drove her crazy in a good way, but she found herself upset by the fact that most of that legend was already uncovered. A similar story in France, however, sent waves of elation down to her core. Making her findings known would give Amanda a huge sense of accomplishment. The words and pictures painted a detailed story of this small ruler. Lamonthe's painting was somewhat decayed by the years but showed a slim-faced man with a long aquiline nose. Bladelike eyebrows and glassy dark eyes were hard to make out from the dried, chipped oil of the tempera. A wide, slanted set of lips above a smooth black goatee fit the typical French duke.

It was nearing five in the evening when Amanda

decided to make some coffee and work a little bit more on this new source. She was tired but too curious to sleep. Lamonthe's name was known, but his story was clouded. The castle's history was mentioned many times under other Norman tyrants and had seen its share of violence, but this was where it started.

Lamonthe was the only son born to a noble house builder and engineer, who aided Louis, Count of Flanders, during the revolt in 1323. Before being imprisoned, Louis granted this man a plot of land west of Crécy if he could make away with a large portion of the wealth from the estate—a move King Charles would make in hopes of weakening the rebellion. Lamonthe senior took this offer and his son, with some Dutch mercenaries, to start construction on the castle. Hugues was twenty when his father died of disease, and Hugues took over from there. His legacy and his father's defection was recognized by King Charles IV, who gave him all the troops he needed to fortify his standing in the north, and he appointed Hugues as duke. He was a successful defender for the people of his realm, and his notoriety was known throughout Normandy.

Amanda kept reading. The tale took a twist when Lamonthe's wife, Catherine, fell ill from the rapid spread of the Black Death, a plague over Europe. The duke's mind left him, day by day, as she lay quarantined in the highest tower. Lamonthe's attention drifted away from the welfare of his people. When she died, he entered into a state of mental decay. He fought off rebelling chiefs and peasants who demanded lower taxes, but the ruler was delirious. The Hundred Years War worked around his immediate region, as the enemy knew of the torturous things he had done to prisoners. Amanda was shocked to see there was no real confirmation on what happened to the duke after that or the men-at-arms under his command.

She sipped her coffee and scrolled down to a 1920s-era photograph of a bearded professor and what looked like an explorer standing in one of the corridors within the castle. Behind them, the hall seemed to have narrowed due to an abrupt ninety-degree cut. In the foreground of the picture, between the two men, was a stone railing that split the room nearly in half.

Why was a railing needed in a room with no drops or gaps? Too many questions, and a disappointing end to a PowerPoint slide. She called Jean to ask about more information, but there was no answer. Amanda got away from the work at hand to rest her weary eyes. She decided to make use of the laundry room downstairs. Her lease was only for a two-month stay, which was fine, as she did not care too much for hotel living. The rain let up as night crept over the town, with some broken-up gray clouds looming before the moon. Amanda decided to call her mom as she waited for her clothes to dry. Just outside the laundry room, she made the call and talked under a light post. The evening air was nice. A couple of bicyclists rode by on the sidewalk and waved to her. There weren't many people outdoors, which gave her privacy on the phone.

"Yeah, I'm fine," she said to her mother. "No, really, I'm okay. It's just France. No, it's not Paris. Don't worry; it's not like I haven't been to another country. This is what I do." She laughed a little as her mom's worried tone crackled through the speaker. "No, I haven't met anyone interesting, I don't really have time."

The narrow one-way street suddenly was illuminated by the headlights of what looked like a van, but the driver inside turned them off. Distant cars and mopeds hummed at the end of the little street. Her mother continued chatting.

"It's good to hear from you too," Amanda said. "I was just checking up on you."

Her mom kept talking, but then one of the washers began wobbling off balance, making an obnoxious banging sound. *Cha-chunk*. Amanda had to conclude the conversation over the phone. She made her way back into the laundry room to silence the noise. Amanda wedged a mop head in between the dancing washer and the stationary one next to it to kill the noise. Afterward, it was too quiet, and she felt disturbed by this odd silence, alone in a laundry room. There was nothing but the steady buzz of the florescent lights. She began stuffing her dry clothes in a bag so she could return to the sanctuary of her apartment room.

Then she froze. The sound of faint shifting of shoes on the tile floor was enough to make her cringe and run for the door, but that all escalated to a heart-pounding flood of fear when a giant wet-gloved hand pressed over her mouth. Even as she tried to scream, her first thought was not of what might happen to her but why the glove was wet. She struggled only for a brief moment.

The damp glove reeked of a heavy, sweet chemical base. Her thoughts and feelings were leaving her, just as the light from the laundry room left her blurred sight.

She knew she was being dragged off by someone with manly strength. The firm grasp of thick arms squeezed her like a boa constrictor, but before she could figure out anything else, cold metal touched her face, and her feet were thrown up. One of her flip-flops went flying off, and the last noise she heard in a rambling of foreign tongue was a loud bang. Then, darkness.

* * *

Earlier that day

The black Audi sedan reflected Don's figure in the gloss of the paint as it pulled up to the front hotel walkway. The window rolled down like in a mobster movie, revealing a neatly groomed man on the inside, wearing a fancy suit and tie. It was Phil Orrelle, grinning delightfully.

"Get in, please. We have much to discuss." he said, sliding across the seat.

Don opened the back seat door and joined the slender man. The driver set off as Phil shook Don's hand and offered him a cigarette.

Don declined but said, "You mentioned a bonus. I'm not sure if I'm eligible for something like that. Not that I'm complaining; who doesn't love money? But I'm just not sure where this is coming from."

Phil smiled. "It's nothing to worry over. The financial turn of events is not that of LPS but basically the result of the fund-raising that's been going on for several months to pay for this project. We got so much that now there is extra. LPS was able to pay for a large part of renewing the site, and the funding from others was more than enough."

Don was confused but liking the thought of it. "So you're giving the leftovers to me … and my team? Why not just save it for the next project?"

The car made a few turns here and there. The traffic was light, and most of the tourists had left the little town of Saint-Lô. The narrow one-way cobblestone streets were the reason why Don could never drive himself around his area of operation.

Phil smiled and replied, "Oh, my good friend, Normandy has seen its share of history. Thanks to organizations like yours, the French people and many in Europe know about our deep roots. It's becoming harder to find new things as we have … dug up everything. I believe with Château Noir Soleil, we have unearthed something grand."

After the sedan made a round-about left turn, Don noticed the small café wedged in with all the other novelty shops and stone buildings. Phil began gossip on another subject when the driver seemed to pass the destination.

Don looked over at Phil, puzzled. "We're still having breakfast, right?"

Phil looked at his driver, pointed with his puny finger, and spoke in French. Don interpreted it as something like, "Hey, you passed it up. Make a U-turn up here." Don really just wanted to get on with his day and shop for his family. There were so many unique little places, but there wasn't enough time to see them all before he had to get back on that plane. However, he also didn't want to disrespect the man who had been so thoughtful toward him. The driver acknowledged the directions and, without a word, spun the car in a 180-degree turn, next to an intersecting alley way. A sudden halt of the vehicle startled both of them, as the stop jerked them forward in their seat. The driver cursed in another language, honking at a cyclist leaving the alley. The car continued its hard turn with haste.

Don's attention was fixed on the maroon-headed pedestrian, but he knew something was wrong when the car's posture seemed to tilt to one side. A rather loud blast shook him to his core, and the driver tried to accelerate but only lost control, veering into a dumpster. Don knew then that someone had shot out the tires. Strangely, the few people in the café and other shops did not seem to mind the noise. Before Don could react, a shard of glass from the window cut into his cheek. The window next to him sustained most of its integrity but was breached by what looked like a small cylindrical projectile that was launched at them from the direction of the alley. The object was already billowing a potent white gas that reached Don's nostrils and eyes as he frantically went for the door handle. The door was still locked from the autolock, and in a panic, he reached for his gun—and realized he had not taken it with him.

Today was his off-day, and for a humble security guard, he didn't feel obligated to carry it. That was a mistake. Now, totally stunned and unaware of his surroundings, he didn't even know if the driver and Phil had made it out. Sounds of ranting voices became stirred, and his eyes were blind to the force that ripped the door open.

The event happened almost instantly. Within thirty

seconds, two men in jumpsuits and black masks pulled Don from the car. The bigger of the two threw Don over his shoulders and retreated into the alley, where they'd left their van, the door already open. The second man kept his gaze on the smoking car and on the people who now began to notice. Don was hurled carelessly into the van, accompanied by the two masked men. The door slid shut, and the big man shouted at the driver. It peeled off in the opposite direction of the alley before anyone made an attempt to call the police.

3

D on remembered the lights flashing. The blinding strobes of white from cameras. He was in between two groups of people who wore police uniforms. It seemed like an illusion, as it all happened so slowly, but as his cognition kicked in, he realized it was his old fellow deputies. They clapped and congratulated him while taking pictures. The press took the snapshots as he marched triumphantly, dressed in his finest uniform for award ceremonies. Ahead was his old chief and the mayor of his old town. What was this? The voices and sounds all seemed so distant. Like a vague dream. Don tried to remember what he'd won or accomplished that was so grand. All he felt was happiness. Then it was all washed away.

What seemed like the longest blackout for Don was actually the least of his trouble. In a bouncing vehicle with duct tape pinching off his nerves around the wrist and ankles, there was no denying that he'd been abducted. The inside of the van was still very dark. No windows at the back and none on the sides. There was only a hint of moonlight shining in from the front windshield, though that was obstructed by a thick mesh cage that separated the driver and passenger cab. A masked man in a gray jumpsuit observed him carefully, with an automatic Uzi on his lap.

How did such a bright day turn around into this? he wondered. Don knew he had worn out his welcome, and all he could think about was his family. The thought of escape would come later. He now had to observe and know his captors, as much as his captors knew him or wanted to know from him.

The gunman was not alone. Apart from the driver and passenger up front was the second masked thug, sitting next to the submachine gun thug. This man was revealed with his white face showing barely in the darkness and his mask pulled over his face. His hand secured a radio. The radio man was chatting in a low voice to somebody about their ETA and checkpoints; police was also mentioned. Then, to Don't surprise, he felt a pair of feet pushed against his. His eyes were still adjusting and continued to burn from the gas, but with closer observation, he noticed another captive in the van with him. A petite figure, bound and gagged as well, but she made no movement.

Don's movement alerted the man with the Uzi. He took one hand off his weapon and banged it against the side of the metal wall to get the other man's attention. The man on the radio stopped to glance at Don with shadows for his eyes. The faint glimmer from the radio switches and lights revealed a square face and little facial hair. He was the larger of the two who had grabbed him. The man's face remained rigid and calm. The two of them made few movements, which seemed somewhat frightening to Don. They were like motionless robots, with every intent to carry out some malicious plot, until the larger man sighed and took off his mask from his bald head. He tossed it off to the side.

Don noticed the rough, downtown British accent when he started to speak. He first thought it was Mark, but the voice was deeper, sharp and unwavering.

"Good morning, chap. Sleep well?"

Don knew he was being coy, but he did not answer. Instead, he countered with a grunt through his gag—a sock stuffed into his mouth with tape securing it.

"I think he wants to say somethin'. Should we let him?" the big man asked the other masked assailant, who remained like a statue. The thug only shrugged in silence. The bald man leaned forward and brought his tone down to a more serious level.

"If I remove your gag, the last thing you want to do is yell, because for one, you're in the middle of nowhere, and two, I'll break your fucking jaw."

The other thug looked over at him, this time with something to say. The masked individual ripped the mask from *her* face, revealing a small, knobby nose with a black nose ring; slim brows complemented by sharp, peering eyes; and tight lips. Her hair was short and unkempt from the sock mask. "We still need him to talk, idiot!" She had attitude to be talking to such a powerful man, but perhaps she was in charge. Her accent was British as well.

The bigger man reassured her with a hand. The van seemed to have transitioned from hard paved road to dirt road at certain intervals. The drive seemed to have gone on for hours, but Don knew nothing of the time or how long he'd been knocked out. The big man reached forward to rip the tape off Don's face. The sting was incredible, but it felt good to breathe out his main windpipe.

"Who the hell are you? What do you want?" Don's questions were the first expected by the thugs.

"Straight to the point; I like that," said the bald man. "You will know soon enough, Mr. Don Millar. Though we ain't giving ourselves away so freely until you do for us first. I don't give a rat's ass about what you want to know about us, but what I do want from you is to be on your best behavior."

Don looked at Amanda Cohen, who lay crunched against the wall at his feet. "Who is she?" he asked.

"She's also going to help us, and with any luck, you two might live through this."

Don didn't like the sound of that. "Where are we going? What time is it?"

The bigger man sat still for a moment. The questions seemed to have pushed him to end the conversation right there. "Jill, shut him up again. I'm done with questions for today."

The woman known as Jill responded to the order and readied a new strip of tape to silence Don. Now more disturbed than ever, Don felt courageous, though in fear for his life. He hadn't been trained in these circumstances. A security guard or head of security was not up to the task of what Navy SEALs are capable of doing in an abduction. What Don did know how to do, however, was scrap.

Jill came forward with the tape as Don waited for her to near. He readied his feet under his bottom. It may have seemed a reckless move, but Don was not taking any chances—he never did. He was about to test the situation. Don's legs propelled his body up like a spring. The top of his head, aimed down like a battering ram, collided with Jill's chest. The sudden tackle pushed her back into her seat, with Don trying to grab at her Uzi with both hands still bound. This obviously reduced his chances of fighting, but in his mind, if he could at least get a weapon in his hands, he might shatter their plans.

The act was pointless. Don felt the surge of pain when Jill lifted her knee up into his groin, followed by another knee to his gut.

"Paul! Get this fucka!" Jill's distress was soon followed by a fierce hand gripping Don's hair and slamming his head into the side of the van door. Paul then gave him a solid fist to the face. Jill, annoyed, kicked Don square in the chin, knocking him back where he was with a loud thud. The beating stopped thereafter. Don had fallen into a state of unconsciousness once more, with a busted lip and purple cheek. The two were not expended at all from the act. It was one out of a thousand times they'd had to deal with resistance. Paul's heavy hit is what put Don to sleep, along with the upper cut to the chin. The driver looked back, with the passenger glaring back as well.

* * *

"You two got everything under control back there?" The voice was French-sounding. The speaker was clean-shaven but had long hair pulled back in a knot. He wasn't too much older than Paul but slimmer and with intensity in the eyes. A dark scar ran vertical near his left ear.

"You check the map?" Paul asked, ignoring the man's question.

The man brought up the GPS with his laptop. "Twenty-five minutes out from the actual site, fifteen from the rendezvous." He directed his attention toward Don. Is he going to be much trouble?"

"Not after that." Paul looked at his watch. "Hopefully I won't have to scuff him up too much. Dumb bastard." He then turned to the man on his laptop. "Daylight is coming soon. We'll get some shut-eye at the safe house, and then hit it." Paul's plan seemed to go without question from the man up front. There was no doubt that Paul was in command. Jill looked over at Paul with concern.

"What about his face? He don't look like he's fit to speak to anyone after that."

Paul glanced back. "You brought your makeup kit, right?"

She nodded. The van followed the snaking road through the countryside and the vast sea of shrubbery. Some parts were thicker than others as they drove past farms and small communities spread out along the highway. "Keep her out. We want our watch to be an easy one," ordered Paul.

Jill stuck Amanda with another sedative drug. Paul was feeling less tense, and reveled the thought of the next big prize. He noticed the vibe in his crew as well and knew it was all downhill from this point on.* * *

The walls all spun around in a dizzy blur. The light from the window was sparse, but there was the first indication of how long it'd been since Amanda was taken. It had been nearly twenty-four hours when she realized she was in a shack out in the country. The new man sitting in front of her was another of the sort like Paul. He held a pump-action shotgun with a bandolier loaded with shells. A vivid and twisted red-purple tattoo crept up his neck and frayed into a spade dragon tail on the side of his face. His hair was buzzed down short in a military fashion. He had a sinister tinge to his eyes. His face was cratered and rough, with a black stubble. She was still bound, but this time in a chair within a dirty room of old brick and mortar. Cobwebs hung from the rafters. Outside, through the window, she could see the French countryside and the thick forest beyond the pasture of grazing cows.

Amanda was next to Don who was also tied up in a chair. She was awake and clearly still shaken from the kidnapping. "Is this a bad dream?" she muttered. *If it is, why am I so cold?*

She was wearing a short-sleeved shirt, cut-off pants, and one flip-flop. Don was in his long-sleeved white shirt and slacks. They had taken his coat to search it.

"Whatever you did in the van, don't do that again," Amanda said to Don. "For your sake."

The man on watch clapped his hands with a grin on his worn face. "Good, good. She's right, you know. Any moves like that, and you're a goner. Especially with me. Jill is a mean bitch, but I'm a different story. You don't want to gamble with us, mate. You'll definitely lose."

"Can I please have a coat? I'm cold," said Amanda in a strained tone.

The guard responded by mocking her. "Eeeewww, I'm

35

cold! I'm a college girl who has no idea where I am, and I'm just so privileged."

"Get her a damn coat, you asshole."

The guard's face twisted in fury. "She's going to have to work for her coat. But as for you, I'm looking for any reason to put you into the ground once we're done here."

Amanda could read Don's anger. Her heart sank.

"I already have a good enough reason to put you in the ground," said Don. The guard racked in a round with a loud *click-clack*.

The sound was so alarming in the quiet room that Amanda winced. Without hesitation, the guard aimed the barrel in Don's direction, and the blast made Amanda's ears ring. The concussion had pound at her soul. Don's chest was pelted with what seemed to be rock salt, as a white cloud of mist lingered where he was sitting. The power of the blast had thrown him backward, and he was now groaning in pain, horizontal in the chair.

The guard was laughing hysterically, a wicked laugh. Amanda could not help but scream. She felt her own scream rather than heard it, as her hearing was impaired. She cried as the guard went on about something. Jill came in through the door in a fury.

"What the fuck, Mav! You trying to decompress his fucking lungs?"

The guard who was called Mav handed her the shotgun as Jill continued to stare him down, expecting an answer.

"My shift is up," he said, irritated, and walked out.

"It's time to go anyway, you wanker!"

Amanda continued to sob, having lost control of her feelings. The whole night was a stir of emotions that she just could not hold anymore. She was not as tough as she had thought. Mav was right—just a college girl.

Jill, being no better, seemed annoyed by Amanda's crying. She grabbed Amanda's long hair and gave her a few slaps on a cheek that was glinting with wet tears.

"Hey! Hey! Shut up! I'm not babysittin' here. I don't need any bitchin' from you." Jill then turned toward Don, still on the floor with the wind knocked out of him. She reached down and lifted him upright. "And you, don't say shit around Maverick, or he'll do some stupid shit you'll regret. Savvy?"

Don's face was sweating from the heavy breathing and all the blood recovering the oxygen from his lungs. His makeup was smudged from when Jill had tried to make him look normal again in the van. He got out a few words to Jill, just as Paul and another woman walked in. "Pl ... please, please ... ge ... get her a coat." Don gestured slightly toward Amanda, who was now much calmer.

Jill turned to Paul for a response. Paul looked at the other woman, who wore an old green military jacket. She had short black hair that didn't go past her neck. She was somewhat taller than Jill and with a slightly thicker body. Her complexion was darker, and she had a sharper nose and jawline. Without a word, she walked out and then back in with a black sports coat that looked like Don's. The darker woman threw the coat at Amanda and covered her only slightly, but was better than nothing. The women made their way around the room as Paul gathered his thoughts.

"While you put yourself together, I'm going to answer the question you asked me last night. Don Millar, you're here to provide me and my team with insurance—insurance to get us in through the checkpoint to Black Sun Castle, and … being that your head of security, your position is what will keep any of your men off the site while we're there, via radio communication. If you try to do anything stupid, like call out for help, I will not hesitate to send you back to your family in pieces."

Don had a feeling they were there for that stupid castle. What it was, he was not sure, but now that this Paul had mentioned his family, Don knew this brigade of thieves was not playing around. Don tried desperately to play it off. "I don't have a family," he said.

Paul got closer and bent down to meet his eyes. "No use in lying, mate. My hacker monitored that call you made to your little wife that night you probably thought there was a power surge. We know where they live, and if you want to let them live, you're going to do as we say. Understood?"

Don nodded and cast a despicable glance at the leader.

Paul smiled in approval. He combed his little goatee and resumed. "Now then, we know of this place LPS has been working on for a while. We know of the gold that is buried there—"

"What? Gold?" Amanda interrupted. "There's no gold there. We surveyed the entire grounds, recovered blueprints. Is … is that what you're after? You kidnapped us to get your hands on something that doesn't exist?"

Paul chuckled and called in his hacker. "Rubio, get in here."

The long-haired passenger from the van stepped in, wearing a turtleneck black sweater with military cargo pants and boots. His long hair was still in a ponytail. He produced a tablet with photos of Jean and Amanda at the café. "We have been watching you, Amanda, for a while," said Rubio. As he scrolled through all of the photos of Amanda's business, Paul went on.

"I'm surprised you have not heard the full story of this asshole who ruled over your precious castle. We saw you analyze the info of this place inside and out. You know a good deal about it; you know the way around it. We know about the treasure inside somewhere, and you're going to help us get to it."

"I don't know where this gold is you're talking about."

Paul looked hard at her. His stare was overpowering as he put his face right up to hers at eye level. "You can damn well figure it out. If not, we're blowing the fucking place down with you in it. Put a big gaping hole in the ground. Now, if you don't want to make a mess of things, it shouldn't be too hard then."

The thought of her work and research gone made her stomach sink. Her life, gone. Amanda wished she had done more research.

Paul looked at Rubio. "Fill her in."

Rubio obliged. "The information we gathered is accurate. It's what we do, but your security has been keeping us locked out of certain information. We know that Hugues de Lamonthe went crazy after losing his wife to the plague. As the main tax collector of the region, he gathered quite a bit of gold and silver, much of it through raiding rebellious villages and strongholds, but the majority was through the king's financing for training more men-at-arms. This was stashed in the castle, perhaps somewhere underground. The main thing here is that when his men tried to turn on him and rob him, he locked himself in with the gold and set everything on fire before the traitors could claim it. The gold has been there ever since. No one attempted to find it after that or even knew about it. The castle itself was not fully claimed by anyone afterward."

Amanda was in shock. "So … you're a bunch of tomb raiders going off—"

"Accurate information," interrupted Paul. He studied both of them carefully. "Helena, untie them. Get her some shoes. From here on out we're at maximum security." He turned to Amanda and Don. "Try anything and … well, you already met Maverick."

The dark, silent woman called Helena retreated from the room to get shoes for Amanda. When she returned, she cut them both free, but they were under constant watch inside the room while the raiders geared up.

It was nearly nine o'clock when they loaded up in the van. In addition to Paul, Jill, Helena, Rubio, and Mav, were two others. A Spanish brute named Alonzo and a husky Russian man called Fang, who was a vicious character with tattoos up and down his bulky arms. He had one good eye, and a glass eye in the right socket. Mav told Don not to act stupid around Fang either, or he would end him, as he'd done to so many when he was locked away in a Russian prison.

Amanda noticed the team was very diverse, and there was probably more of them. More contacts in other countries. Their gear and equipment spoke for itself. They had assault weapons, explosives, riot gear, and satellite communications equipment. If she got back from all this, she was going to give LPS a piece of her mind and demand answers as to what was not shared.

Amanda was just as clueless as Don, but she had to pull herself together, or she'd be buried with Lamonthe's burnt remains. The six of them rode in the van while the other three took a separate car. Amanda and Don were given some crackers and water to keep them alive. Helena and Alonzo kept watch on them in the back while Jill drove and Paul observed in the passenger seat. Don was chewing on his salty cracker when a thought came to his head. He looked at Alonzo.

"When you nabbed me, why just me? Did you have any clue who was in that car with me?"

"Orrelle is useless to us," Alonzo answered. "He doesn't know the security like you do. Even if we had him as a hostage, he couldn't communicate with your men."

That made sense to Don, especially since Phil had no say or command of security. To control the circus, you needed the ringleader, not the clown.

"They're gonna be looking everywhere for me," Don insisted. "What makes you think those guards are going to remain calm when they see me? I'll be all over the news."

Alonzo looked at Helena, who remained silent. He then looked at Don as he washed his cracker down with water. "You Americans think you're so popular. What makes you think Orrelle is still alive?"

Don considered the question as self-explanatory. He

wasn't sure, but guessing by Alonzo's demeanor, they'd killed Phil and his driver in that car. Don looked at Amanda. "Hey, you gonna be okay?"

She gave him a hopeless glance. "Silly question to be asking right now."

Don felt stupid at that. "You know they just want this gold, is all, not us. We play it cool, and we'll be fine," he said, reassuring her.

Amanda nearly cracked a smile. "You think they'll actually let us go after seeing all this? I don't know about you, but I'm dead if I don't find that gold. These people are crazy."

"But they aren't so stupid as to leave bodies, and they can disappear wherever. There's no use in killing us."

"Enough chatter," snapped Helena. The tough woman wielded an HK G36 carbine rifle. Don didn't know why— *It's not like the LPS security team are soldiers*—but he knew his men would put up a fight, especially if they knew he was a hostage. He prayed it wouldn't come to that.

They stopped alongside the dirt road. Jill got out and walked around to open the sliding door. She pointed to Don. "You, come out; move your ass."

Don did as he was told. When he got out, he saw Rubio setting up some sort of device at the back of the little car. A small satellite array was placed on the roof with wires running to the trunk. Don guessed that they were on the highway running south. They were very close to the main checkpoint, which as just up ahead.

Paul got out, but instead of being strapped in gear, he wore a gray button-up shirt tucked into black pants, and a company hat with an IT logo stitched into the fabric.

Don then realized he was dressed as an LPS technical associate.

"Pretty accurate, yeah? Today you will be escorting me onto the premises to reclaim the security equipment. Otherwise, why would they think you would need a giant-ass van? I will ride up front with you. Do all the talking; they know you."

Mav and Fang loaded into the van. Rubio followed, abandoning the car.

"Sensors are on and will detect passing squad cars if we get company. Let's make this quick," said Rubio.

Paul looked at Don. "You heard him. Don't fuck it up. Get in the driver's seat."

A number of scenarios ran through Don's head. Being the driver of the top-heavy van, he considered cranking the steering wheel hard right to roll the vehicle. Then he thought of how the action might hurt Amanda or even kill her. He also thought of his family and returning home alive, which soon vanquished those thoughts of being a hero. He had to remind himself he was not a cop anymore.

4

Don controlled his breathing as he turned the van onto the gravel road. The checkpoint booth was up ahead, with the fifteen-foot razor-wire fence securing the flanks. He feared that if his men caught on, Paul's brigade would lay waste to them. The van came to a halt before the striped lift arm.

A guard in a black uniform with cap and sunglasses stepped out of the booth. He smiled, already recognizing Don. "How we doing today, sir? Were we expecting anything today?"

Yeah, a robbery. Don showed him his badge to set the example, as always. "Oh, just taking a cruise with my tech buddy here. Nothing too major. I have to show him where the cameras are for disassembly. Gonna be packing up this place soon." Don handed him Paul's alias badge. The guard studied the badge for a brief moment and scanned Paul into the system.

Paul knew that Rubio had thought of that in advance and slipped in the alias using Don's breached network. He kept calm, with a grin.

Don, however, had to wipe the sweat from his brow and kept his face to the front, but the guard had already seen the bruise on Don's face.

"You okay, sir? You look like you had a rough night."

Don faked a laugh. "It's fine. I collided with a cyclist yesterday. You know how they are around here."

The guard smiled and handed them back their badges. "Yeah, the French are something else. Have a good day, sir." The guard gave him a sort of salute wave. The two other guards at the checkpoint waved from within the large office next to the booth. The hard part was over. The van made its way past outer security and into the shade of the tall pines and brush. The sky overhead was darkening with clouds, and the wind picked up, stirring the dead leaves across the rocky road.

After a few minutes, Paul ordered the van to stop. He looked into the dim forest surrounding them and then at Don. "I know you have men on the site and cameras. Rubio is going to do his magic, but he needs the IP address to the network. What is it?"

Don gave him the numbers, and Rubio punched them in. "There are only two men on site today," said Don. "Usually they just keep to the outside walls."

Paul gave him the radio. "Call them off."

Don had a hard time processing that ploy. "And tell them what? It's their shift today. They would suspect something."

Paul was getting irritated. "Tell them to take the day off to compensate them for a job well done. Otherwise, we will use our own methods."

"Jesus! Okay, just ... hold on." Don took a deep breath. He switched to the right channel and called out to the team.

A faint response came in and became clear the second time. "Go ahead, Mr. Millar," came the sharp response.

"Hey, Sam, you guys can take the day off—let Mike know as well. Go enjoy yourselves. I'll be on the site for most of the day."

There was a moment of silence. "Copy, sir, but what about Louis? He had inner guard today. Over."

Don felt the knot tighten in his gut—that unpleasant feeling of raw fear, of knowing just who is going to react to a mistake, and it was Mav, in the seat behind him. A fist clenched onto Don's hair, nearly pulling it from his scalp. A cold metal gun barrel pressed into his cheek.

"My boss asked you how many men were on today, and you gave him a horse-shite answer! I say we put another good beating on him, Paul. He obviously ain't learned his lesson yet."

Paul dismissed Mav's reaction. "Why didn't you tell me of this man on shift? I need full accountability." Don didn't want to answer, but then Paul lost his patience and had Rubio hand him the laptop. Paul pulled something up on the screen as he talked. "Millar, you are one dumb wanker. I want to show you that we are not your average criminals. I have little tolerance with people who don't cooperate." Paul swiveled the screen around to show Don a live camera feed of his house back in the States.

Don was enveloped in pure rage, knowing these animals had eyes on his family.

"I'll bet you want to see them again. Look here," said Paul, zooming in on the window.

Don saw his wife inside, doing the dishes. With that, Don was relieved—they hadn't been hurt, but he had to play it cool for now. "Look, I'm sorry. I forgot about him. Most times we only have two on."

Paul noticed a follow-up call coming in over the radio. "Sir? Mr. Millar, come in."

Don replied. "Hey, Sam. Yeah, tell Louis as well. Good job this month."

"Copy that. Thanks, sir."

Don continued driving down the winding road for another two minutes until they finally came upon a large grassy clearing—an area carved out from the forest, the size of two football fields. The castle was bleak against the shadows of the trees that were not too far from the outer walls. It sat unwavering and solid in the wind.

Rubio gave Paul the situation on the surveillance. "Cameras are still active, with two-minute loop feed. They won't know were here."

"Good. Millar, stop here," ordered Paul. The van pulled off to the side once more. Up ahead were the security trucks and maintenance equipment, fifty yards from the front portcullis gate. Don spotted two of the guards. Sam and Mike stepped out of the small trailer office with their lunch bags and other bits of gear.

"I don't see the third one, Millar," said Paul.

Don tried to reassure Paul that Louis was on his way out, but Paul made him radio again. There was no response, and Don assumed they must have put away their radios.

"Why isn't Louis on his radio, Millar?"

"He probably set it down somewhere and forgot it; he's like that. Just give it a minute. He'll be out."

Another minute passed. Mike got into a truck and

started off. He spotted the van as he was pulling out. Mike stopped next to Don's van and rolled down the window. Don did the same.

"Thanks for the day off, sir. It was getting pretty damn boring. Louis rode with Sam."

"I hear ya. Take it easy, Mike." The guard nodded and sped away.

Sam had his attention on the van now as he waited patiently for Louis. Sam then walked toward the van.

"Go. Meet him halfway," Paul ordered.

Don pulled the van up to Sam, who smiled and waved at Don.

"Mr. Millar, how you doing? You got IT doing updates?" Sam pointed at Paul who was secretly twisting a suppressor on his Glock 40.

"Oh yeah, just running the tests on the cams and what-not. Where's Louis? I couldn't get him on the radio."

Sam shrugged and looked back toward the castle. "Probably set his radio down somewhere. I'll run in there to fetch him." Sam gestured to his own face. "Jesus, Mr. Millar, what happened right here?"

"A little accident with a biker. Can you check on Louis?" Don ended the conversation quickly.

Sam nodded awkwardly and made his way back to the castle.

Don pulled the van up closer to the castle and waited.

"This is becoming too much of a wait," Jill said from the back. "We need to get in there and ice them."

Paul looked at her dumbfounded. "And risk two of them getting wind of us and then radioing in for help? We fucking wait, okay, for them to come back out in daylight."

"Please don't hurt them. They're good guys. They'll leave," pleaded Don.

"You better hope they do." Paul turned around and studied Amanda, who was trembling from the suspense. She didn't know where the gold was, and her only hope was getting the attention of the guards. It was that or be killed. Then, from behind the opened portcullis gate, Sam rushed out. A sense of urgency was on his face as he pointed back toward the castle's chapel entrance.

"Millar, something's happened to Louis! Come quick! I don't know what's going on!"

Don heard Jill and a couple of others in the back curse and mumble at the setback. Don reached for the door, but Paul grabbed him.

"Hold up. I'm coming with." Paul looked at everyone else. "You all stay here while I figure out what the bloody hell's going on." The two rushed in after Sam.

They were in the front courtyard, which was overlooked by the colossal cathedral that acted as the castle's religious hub in the fourteenth century. The twenty-foot double doors made of wood and iron were open as Don and Paul rushed in. The interior was filled with oak benches, holy water shrines (now empty), and a dim light that filtered through the stained-glass windows in the slightest way. Sam managed to assist Louis to the front podium and kneeling steps of the gothic interior. Louis had one arm over Sam. The expression on Louis's face seemed frozen. His skin was clammy and pale. His knees seemed weakened by something that hindered him from walking straight. Don noticed that although the interior was cold, Louis was sweating.

"Good God, what's wrong with him?" Paul asked; he seemed genuinely surprised.

Louis grabbed onto a replica candle stand but knocked it over and frantically tried to grip at Sam's collar. Saliva oozed from his mouth.

"He had a seizure. Found him at the bottom level of the main tower. He said he saw something, a man in black robes."

"I thought he was alone in here," said Don.

"He was. I called Mike back over here. We're going to comb through the site."

Don lay Louis on his side and propped his head up on his own jacket while Louis slowly sank into unconsciousness.

"Shit," said Don. "What else did he say when you saw him?"

Sam looked worried. "He said there was a man in black. Pointing at the floor was all I got. You want to stay with him? I think I hear Mike out there."

"Why would somebody walk around here with black robes?" asked Paul as Sam left.

"I don't know! Sometimes punks end up sneaking on the site and do stupid things."

"Fuck, either you have something going on here, or your man is a junky. Now we're going to have to deal with these people if they won't leave."

Outside Sam waved at Mike who pulled up behind the van and rushed out.

"Damn, is he okay?"

"Yeah, it was just a minor seizure, but whatever he saw

spooked him. We need to secure the area just in case," said Sam, drawing out his compact pistol.

Amanda was finished with waiting. She had to make an attempt to get the guard's attention, even if it cost her. She was a goner anyway.

"*Help! Help!* They're killers!" she screamed as she banged on the side of the van. The guards were startled by this, thinking that Don had brought only one other person.

Helena used the hard stock of her carbine to bash Amanda in the face. The impact was enough to silence and daze her.

The two guards knew what was going on in the van, and they focused their pistols on the sliding door.

"Whoever is in the van, come out with your hands showing. Slowly!" shouted Sam. He then reached for his radio to call in a quick report but was stopped by a blind volley of fire that kicked up the mud around them. The muffled automatic pops from Helena's and Alonzo's rifles were heard as the rounds tore through the metal. A bullet met with Mike's shin as they both returned fire with their side arms and retreated backward. Mike grimaced and stumbled onto his back.

"Mike!" Sam shot two more times at the van before his clip ran out. Helena threw open the sliding door and unloaded a quick burst into Sam. The rounds to the chest threw him back and killed him. Mike, who was still on the ground, helplessly fired back with a fresh clip, landing the two shots in Helena's chest. She also was thrown back from the impact. Paul rushed to the front entrance and steadied his Glock on Mike, who managed to get back to his feet and took shelter behind a giant generator. Maverick and Alonzo returned fire upon the generator but had no clear shot.

"*No!*" Don swept up from behind, knocking Paul off balance. The shot veered off. Paul tried to recover from the tackle and unleashed a kick into Don's gut. Don went for a punch to the groin, but Paul caught that and hit him over the head with his pistol handle. Mike then aimed at Paul. He shot, but missed. Don heard the zip and pop of the bullet digging into the stone archwork behind him. Paul was quicker with his gun and landed one in Mike's chest, finishing him with one in the head. A small red dot on his light skin confirmed it as he fell back to the mud. Helena recovered and got out of the van, trying to catch a breath from the two slugs that lodged into her vest armor. At this point everyone got out of the van to better observe the roadway leading in.

"Fucking hell! What was that?" shouted Paul. Jill grabbed the radio off Sam, the same radio that he'd gotten from Louis.

"The bitch squeaked; got their attention. They would have been gone if it wasn't for the cheeky bastard in there. What's going on with that, huh?" The radio crackled in her hand.

"Sam? Sam, come in. This is guard shack. Mr. Millar?"

"Shit ..." Jill tossed the radio to Paul.

He kept calm and replied, "Guard shack, this is Bryman with IT. Go ahead."

"Uh, yeah, we heard shots over there, just wanting a report. Can you put Millar or Sam on, please?"

Don knew he had to reply or things could get much

worse. Paul handed him the radio. "Tell them you guys were fooling around. Do it, or I swear it all ends now."

Don reluctantly spoke into the radio. "Yeah, sorry if that startled you guys. We were just having some target practice."

"Uh, copy. Thought we heard some automatic fire. You got sparklers going off?"

Paul glared at Don with an icy stare and centered his gun on Don's bloody head, droplets falling onto the dark stone steps. "Make it sound convincing this time!"

Don nodded and replied, "Yeah, I brought over some special pieces of hardware; just don't tell. I have friends with the local SWAT teams around here. Thought we'd pass the time." For a moment there was silence. Don hoped they wouldn't come over; it would be certain death if they did.

Finally, a reply: "Hey, no problem, sir. Stay safe. Over and out."

Paul secured the radio again and told Mav to hide the bodies. Fang helped out.

Jill asked again. "So what the hell happened in there?"

"Don't worry about it. Just get her secured and look out for this prick. I got to check up on the mental case." Paul walked back into the cathedral but found nothing. Louis was gone.

5

manda was thrown from the van. Helena did not go soft on her after her last act. Amanda recovered herself from the mud. She could feel the cut just under her left eye where the butt stock struck her. She used her sleeve to soak up the blood and tried not to cry. She reminded herself of who she was and what she stood for as she gazed at the castle standing in absolute beauty. The corbels that supported the battlements on the walls were the same bladelike wedges that gave the architecture a twisted and rather intimidating look.

The black stains from the boiling tar that was used to pour on attacking Englishmen were still there cascading from under the machicolations. Loophole-like windows followed the inside spiral stairs of the two hexagonal watchtowers on either end, through which archers fired. The left wall that extended out to the south side was at a diagonal angle as opposed to being at a flat ninety degrees from the joining wall, as if the structure were built to deflect incoming cannon balls. Amanda knew that was strange being, as forts were not built like that until gunpowder cannon was used in the late fifteenth century. Star-shaped forts were built with a series of sharp corners and angled vertical walls. Black Sun was very close to the concept.

All this foolishness of thinking about her death didn't bother her now. She would die a victim. The case would be long investigated by hundreds of angry French officials. She was sure that wasn't what Paul wanted either. Amanda reflected on Don's words. To her it seemed Paul's crew needed to finish off a job clean, even if someone had to die from recklessness.

The crew walked up the few steps leading up to the goliath double doorway of the eastern cathedral. The vast, dark interior was enough to baffle Paul's team. It was the instant solitude that stirred the nerves under the skin. The pews were aligned properly, polished, and on either side of the stone aisle. Up front was the altar and organ pipes, stretching up the back wall. Just to the right was the small organ room. Some utilities were present for restoration—a tool bag here, a step ladder there. Paint buckets and stone preservatives had been left in some corners. The organ was clearly new and had been added as a bonus, like everything else in the castle.

Paul was having a hard time taking in the sights. He pointed in the spot where Louis had been. The guard who had had a critical seizure only moments ago was gone.

"He was just here. What the hell happened?"

Mav looked at him strangely. "The fuck, you mean? Who was that?"

Paul waved his hand gun around. "The bastard who had a seizure five minutes ago! Shit, I took my eyes off him to save your asses! You"—he pointed to Helena and then to Alonzo—"and you, go check that room in the far corner and whatever is behind that door. Don't go too far. He had to have gone further in. Careful; he's still armed."

"You didn't grab his gun?" said Jill.

Paul sensed he was being judged for his slipup. "I would have if you all would have handled this shithead in the van! He doesn't have a radio, so he can't call out, but we can't let him leave alive." He took a breath and passed his fingers over the top of his shaved head.

Helena dragged open the solid wood door to the small organ room, and the sound echoed. Alonzo checked behind the door straight back, leading further into the castle.

"I need to get those cameras up, our cameras," said the tech Rubio. Paul gave him the clearance, and Rubio went back out to set up their over watch.

Paul glared at Amanda. "So now it's your turn. Is there any other entry or exit into the walls?"

Amanda was straight with him. "Yes, there's the northwest gate, but that's usually closed. The exhibit—"

"I don't give two shits about the exhibit. What about the inner walls? Any breaches, gaps?" barked Paul.

"No, we patched up most of it. Some cosmetic damage is left, but it's a solid structure."

"You have the blueprints saved in a file?"

"I do." Amanda was nervous she would utter something that he did not want to hear. *This man is driven mad with greed*, she thought.

Jill grabbed the tough industrial laptop sitting next to some of Rubio's hardware. "Log into LPS. Bring it up. I'll be watching," said Jill, handing Amanda the computer.

While Amanda was accessing her account, Don

glared at Paul. "Those were men with families out there. You killed them."

Paul chuckled and leaned in. "We all have families. Why do you think we're here mate? You just better hope yours is safe if something happens to us. You know your friend can't get too far. We have it covered. If there's any place he could hide, she will tell me." Paul then walked over to Jill who was looking at Amanda's account. "Speaking of which, what do we have?"

The screen brought up the layout of the castle—every door, window, and wall; the bottom floor, the second, and the tower rooms, including the eight guard towers. Just behind the narrow welcoming hall of the chapel was the main courtyard. Outside to the left, on the north end, were the stables, and opposite that was the training yard on the south side, with the pond and gardens adjacent to that.

Everything else in the middle was part of the interior chambers and rooms. Paul brought up his radio and flipped to their frequency. "Rubio, come in." Rubio responded. Paul gave him orders to go up the northern guard walls through two of the towers to place a camera overlooking the northwest gate. He also noticed the two-story barracks that were detached from the main body of the castle, just above the gardens to the south. "Place one in there as well. I want this place wrapped up tight."

"Copy."

Paul then called out to Helena and Alonzo. "How we looking on finding that stray?"

Alonzo came on with his Spanish accent. "Nothing

so far. We searched the courtyard and the stables but no sign. This opposite gate is locked shut."

Mav turned to Paul. "You don't think … the poor bastard jumped? You know, from the wall?"

Amanda answered for him. "The walls are forty feet high. If he did, he's not getting back up after that fall."

Mav grunted. "Hmm, it's a shame. All right, where's this damn room, then?"

"What room?" asked Amanda.

Jill became annoyed and pointed at the screen. "Show us where the fucking room with the gold is!"

"Jesus, I told you—"

Paul raised his pistol to her head. "And I told you to get your shit together and find us the room, or you die knowing nothing about this gothic torture chamber!"

"Okay! Just let me think!"

"Clocks ticking, Cohen." Rubio had walked in through the door just left of the altar.

"Get the feed up," commanded Paul.

Amanda thought of everything, even the hidden passageway leading from the upper servants' quarters to the lower servants' rooms. Then it hit her—the research Jean had sent her. The room with the stone hand railing dividing one-half of the room. That was it.

"There's a way to a sublevel. I didn't know at first, but it's under the Weeping Tower," said Amanda.

"Show us," said Paul. "Helena, Alonzo, meet us in the center courtyard." He looked down at Don. "We're going for a stroll." The team collected their gear and weapons. The hall behind the cathedral was lined with wide arched windows looking out onto the bleak cobblestone courtyard. On their left were the stairs to the northern part of the wall. To the right was another wood and iron door. Fang tried opening it, but it was locked.

"That's to the old guard's mess hall. We can go through the great hall. This way," said Amanda, stepping into the courtyard where Alonzo and Helena met after searching the stables. Mav stared in awe at the statue erected from the center of the yard—a woman kneeling with what looked to be a sword or weapon of some sort—it had been broken off many years ago. Amanda recalled the excellence of the piece as well, despite the nicks and wear over the centuries. The woman's robe retaining the folds in the etched stone were thoughtfully chiseled and smoothed. Protruding from her back were wings, but one wing was the shape of an angel's, with feathers carved precisely along the wing blade. The other wing was somewhat stained black but resembled a bat's or demon's wing, with the hook-like claw at the joint.

"This place was here for how long? How does it look so intact? We thought it would be only a few walls left standing," said Jill, looking around.

"That's what puzzled us. We were led to believe that Lamonthe used the finest building materials. The French also maintained it to some degree, but still ..."

Mav pointed up to the tower that seemed to go above the tops of the tall pines surrounding them.

Fang was feeling up for conversation. His baritone voice was rough and heavy with a Russian accent. "I read the history of this place in a World War Two memoir from an American fighter pilot. He mentioned how two bombs leveled this place after they spotted a Nazi squad fleeing inside. This castle should be erased."

Amanda was familiar with that story as well, but never believed it. "Most of it was still standing when we found it. Not sure how that is possible," she said. "Our guess is the French populace or even low-funded private parties attempted to build a little bit more as time went on, but the patterns of the stones all seem consistent with each other and are cut the same."

"And that?" said Jill, looking up.

"The Weeping Tower. Lamonthe and his wife's quarters. It's also where she lay sick for weeks before dying of the plague. Lamonthe grieved by her side, hence the name. It was also built that high to look out past the dense vegetation." Amanda knew it must have led to further violence once it was over for Lamonthe's wife. Her last experience with the place was a bit unsettling, due to the history and the general vibe of the castle itself.

They filed in through the door on the left, entering the great hall or throne room. The room was decorated with strips of red carpet on either side of the small table used for council meetings. On the far opposite ends of the room were stone pillars, set three yards apart, that supported the vaulted ceiling, which rose up to twenty feet. The little daylight there was crept in through the left side windows.

Their footsteps could be heard throughout the room, amplified as they were by the acoustic nature of the high ceiling. Also to the left was a set of stairs going up, but the team stayed on course and headed right for the kitchen. Adjacent to the kitchen was the servants' dining area.

The team hooked another right with a set of stone stairs leading directly ahead.

"To the left are the bottom-floor rooms of the servants' quarters. This is the base of the tower." Amanda stepped off further to the right to inspect the area. She was in the room with the stone railing in the center. The door ahead of her was to the west end of the guards' mess hall. The floor next to the railing had to have been put in after the original build. She knelt down and saw a slight difference in the stone from the oldest to most recent. The older stone was smoother and worn down. A slight crease in the floor lined up with where the stone railing ended.

"This is it. Someone had covered it up! Oh my God, I can't believe I missed this. There must have been stairs leading down right here."

Paul looked over the small portion of the floor.

"Well, Mav, what do you think? Can you blow through it?"

Mav nodded. "Not sure how many layers of brick have been placed, but if I can direct the explosive downward we should be good."

"And make a hell of a lot of noise. We already pressed our luck with gunshots; now we're going to be blowing shit up?" Helena objected.

"Stay in your own damn lane. Let me do my job. It's going to be a slight bump in the ground. According to our tour guide, there's another layer of wall after this one, so noise shouldn't be a problem." Mav took out a brick of shaped C4 and placed it on a nearby crate. He began sorting out the shock tube and blasting caps.

"No, she's right. I'm not risking that any more of those

bastards will come over," said Paul. He could see that Mav was already turning red but quickly thought of an idea. Paul held the radio to Don. "You're up! Tell the guards that a group of miners are using demolitions. Tell them not to worry," demanded Paul.

Don was dumbfounded. "Miners in this area? There's nothing to mine—"

"Let's not overthink things, Millar!" Paul's shouts persuaded Don to grab the radio.

He paused to think about how he would say it in a manner that would convince the guards. "Guard shack, this is Millar."

"Millar, this is guard shack. Go ahead."

"Hey, I just met some contractors a few miles north of the site. They're going to be moving earth around. The big man said it's nothing too dangerous and that they have all the credentials with county clearances. There's going to be some booms; don't be alarmed. Over."

The gang was in complete suspense, holding their breath. Don's hands were sweaty holding the radio.

The reply came. "Okay, like mining?"

"Yeah, excavating for minerals. They're trying to get through the bedrock," said Don, already confident.

"All right, boss, no worries. Guard shack out."

Paul snatched back the radio and looked to Mav. "That's our cue. There's no one else who will call in the noises. Rubio checked for farms and homes earlier, and there's none within thirty-six miles of here. What else do we need?"

"I need a hole dug smack dab in the center, a foot and a half down. Use that pick ax."

Paul grabbed the pick ax hanging from Mav's backpack and tossed it at Don.

"You heard him. Start digging."

Don wanted to take the ax and bury it in Paul's head, but that was not the call to make now. He chipped away at the stone for quite some time. When he got tired, Fang pushed him aside and took over.

"We're on the clock," Fang growled.

When Don sat down against the wall to rest, Paul asked him a question. "Your man, Louis. Is he delirious? On medication?"

"You mean from the seizure?"

"Yeah, and what he said about that other man he saw in here, someone in black robes. You know anything about that?"

"No, I don't. He is usually fine. Always seemed normal around us. He's not stupid; he won't attack you if you're in a group. There's no use in tracking him down. Just let him be."

"He's a liability. I'll do what I have to do."

Fang's strikes to the floor came to a stop. A narrow slot in the busted stone was big enough for the cylindrical explosive Mav had shaped with his hands in order to fit. A blasting cap wedged in the top sprouted a shock tube cord linked to a manual detonator.

"All right, you cheeky dopes. Find cover. I'm breaching," warned Mav, reeling out the detonation cord. Everyone stepped back behind the other set of stairs around the corner. "Fire in the hole!" With a twist, the cord snapped and whistled. *Boom!* Dust clouds filled the air and choked Amanda, who was not prepared for it. A heart-crushing blast was loud enough to ring eardrums but still was muffled to where it would not be heard from too far off.

The sound of rocks falling meant there was a hole. They all saw that the breach was a success, with only five layers of brick running deep and most of it eroded by the damp soil and roots that had weaved through over the years. The dust began to settle as Fang used the pick ax to knock out some of the resisting stones and bricks that jutted out for a full opening into a black abyss.

A smile crept over Paul's face. "We're golden now, mates. Who's first?"

Jill forced an LED light into Amanda's hand and waved her Uzi in the direction of the basement. The air hit her nostrils as cold and damp. It reeked of death and mildew. The light pierced through like a laser beam, revealing the walls and floors with some stone and wood beams intact. The team descended the chipped stairs cautiously, fearing they might stumble. More beams of light shone through and landed on some shelves and racks with giant barrels. Some were rotted and busted open, but four remained.

"The barrels must be wine or mead of some sort," said Amanda.

Mav shoved his combat knife into the first barrel and pried it open a little to let out the sour wine. He sniffed at it on his finger.

"Very bitter, tart wine, I think. It's a shame. I was needing something to take the edge off."

Helena had to quip, "Ha, you feeling shaken up already, Nancy?"

"This place ain't the fucking Hampton Inn. Don't know about you, but I want to get this shit done, sweetheart."

Up ahead was another darkened opening, and behind them was a wood door that looked rotted. Amanda pointed at the door. "I'm not sure about this layout, but we should see if that leads to anything."

Paul gestured for Fang to take care of the door. The burly man kicked and made short work of the splintered wood. The team moved into what looked like a shorter room with devices that sent a shudder through Amanda. Several torture instruments and pieces of equipment were found, either broken or standing upright, retaining a rusted form from the years. Chains with hooks hung from the ceiling, with the cobwebs stretched in between.

To the right were two cages—prisoner cells. No skeletons were left inside, but tick marks were found etched into the stones. Another door was ahead, this one made of stern wood and steel bracing. Amanda pulled at the ring but the door would only budge an inch. Don came behind to help as they both pulled together in unison. The door cracked and flew open. A gust of cold-smelling air wafted through the room. Amanda was amazed. The room was smaller but curved in a half crescent. More shelves and dilapidated wooden tables lined the wall with books, and rippled brown-paper notes were strewn everywhere.

"*Dios mio,*" gasped Alonzo. He made the sign of the cross over his head and chest as the team glanced at a pentagram with several skulls at their feet. Amanda knelt down to see that it had been stained onto the rock using some sort of acid. The leather-bound book on the desk was the first thing that called out to her. Melted candles were everywhere among the cobwebs and books.

"You mind telling me what kind of sorcerer lived here?" asked Paul.

Amanda flipped through the dusty pages. She looked up around the walls and shook her head in pure bafflement. "I have no idea, but if I had to guess, this was Lamonthe's private study."

"As long as he was a rich sorcerer, I don't give two fucks about all this voodoo. We still got that other way to check out. It's a dead end here," said Jill.

Amanda turned to Paul. "I can probably find out more about the location of the treasure and more if you leave me here to look. There must be more maps. There is too much here to pass up."

"By yourself? Fang, you stay with her while she does more homework. But if we get caught at a fork, we're coming back here got it? No funny business."

Amanda was grateful for at least that much. If she could spend another day down there without a gun at her back, she'd be overwhelmed with excitement. Who knew what went on within the mind of the French duke. So far, it wasn't anything good.

Alonzo Ortega gripped his crucifix in his sweaty palm. The musty cold air was alien to him, despite having been in other places around the world. He mumbled a short prayer in Spanish as the piercing lights danced across the black walls. The breath from the rest of the crew could be seen venting from their mouths. The next passage after the wine cellar was even denser with the smell of the dead. Their lights unveiled large indentions in the walls on either side of them.

"Catacombs," blurted Don. The team slowed down unintentionally. Paul and his gang had been through crypts before, but no matter how many times they entered a place of skeletal remains, a slight of hesitation always got the better of them. Mav withdrew a filtered mask from a pouch and stretched it over his head. Helena did the same.

Jill cursed. "Shit, I forgot my damn mask!"

Paul tossed his to her. "Here. I breathed enough of this shit in Syria, and I'm still alive. It's a different story if their rotting."

Rubio handed Paul a bandana. "I take it you don't know about the bacteria that survive in a damp atmosphere like this. Bodies or no bodies."

Paul took his word for it and tied the bandana around his mouth. Don was concerned that he didn't get a mask. *The untold amount of residual plague that looms down here surely will play a number on my health,* Don thought, *if a bullet doesn't by the end of all this.*

"Some of them still have original plate armor. We should bag that too. Knight's armor is worth a pretty penny to collectors," Helena said.

Somebody had brushed past one of the skeleton arms. The whole bony body slipped out from its sockets and rattled to the floor. The lights fell on Alonzo with a look of accidental guilt on his face.

"Sorry," he said. Paul shook his head and glanced back at Jill, who was examining one of the dead knight's helmets. Paul grabbed it from her and tossed it back in the alcove where it banged against more bones.

"We keep to the main prize at hand. Then we come back for the armor."

Alonzo spoke up from the back of the file. "We shouldn't molest the dead," he said. "We never do."

"They don't need the shit anymore, Alonzo. Bugger off!" shouted Jill.

Alonzo uttered something again in Spanish that no one really cared to hear. The long dusty hall began to wind around to the right. Alonzo spotted old torches nestled in the wall brackets. He brushed away some cobwebs and felt the frayed fibers of wood.

"Still oily," he said as he took out a lighter and lit the torch. The fire came to life. Mav did the same to the torch on the opposite wall. The light flickered and revealed the last segment of the dreaded hall. Don noticed a small puddle off to the right and drops of water forming at the rocky ceiling. To the far left of the wide hall was a larger body of water from the leaking. A part of the walkway was flooded, but accessible.

"Water? From where?" asked Paul.

"Most likely from the garden pond just above us," said Don.

They heard the drops every thirty seconds. The next hall was narrower and better built. More stone encompassed the walls and ceiling, but a certain segment was off. Mav lit the next set of torches on either side of the discolored brick.

"See here—dead end, but this wall looks like it was crudely built in a hurry. Alonzo …" Paul motioned for his help to muscle a heavy blow in the wall with the pick. A good chunk flew out from the point, but the wall sustained. Mav prepared a bit of plastic explosive.

"Careful with this one. We don't want the whole foundation tumbling down on us," said Paul. The small cube of C4 was fixed to an end of a pole Mav found near one of the alcoves. He wired another two at the base of the wall with some damp mud tamped over it. The team drew back into the catacombs as Mav unreeled the shock tube.

"Firing!" Another snap, and a greater whiff of cold decay lifted around them as the blast tore through the wall, throwing chips of stone and rock everywhere. The explosion only shook the walls slightly. Paul was relieved the ceiling didn't cave in, as it had happened once before in Egypt. The new smell of rotted air flooded in as the crew entered the next chamber. They quickly escaped the cloud of dust by rushing through it. What really hit them next was everything Paul was looking for—the prize.

6

Jill was breathless as she fell back against the wall in disbelief. After Don fanned more of the dirt from his face, he saw it there. The lights offered a glimpse of gold and silver coins. Plates, chalices, as well as a few jewels. Under their masks, smiles crept across their faces as they looked at one another. Paul walked up to the giant pile in the center of the chamber and shined his light farther in. The old treasury vault was long and supported with four stone pillars. He also noticed some of the gold in the center was melted together. On each pillar, skeletal remains were still hanging in shackles, facing the center of the room. On top of the melted gold were two other blackened-bones skeletons.

The image was ghastly, and there was another giant black stain of something that circled the skeletons. In the center of the gold pile was a stained pentagram and other unusual markings in what looked like ink or blood. The gold was piled knee-high.

"What do you think happened?" asked Helena.

Paul shook his head. "That's what Miss Cohen is finding out. On the other hand …" Paul turned around and pulled the bandana from his mouth, revealing a grin from cheek to cheek. "We're all fucking rich!" He burst into peals of laughter

Jill laughed, and Helena beamed with joy. Mav slapped Paul on the back and congratulated him and then around for Alonzo. He was in the corner of the chamber.

"Oy! Al, we got it. What you doing over there, shriveled up in the corner?"

The Spanish gun hand looked clammy and shook his head as he held his rosary close to his heart. "This place is evil. We need to leave." He pointed to the stain of the star on the dusty treasure.

Mav chuckled and threw his arms up. "All right, ol' boyo, we'll leave as soon as we get this gold. You want to help out or stand there and whimper?"

Then all was quiet. The celebrating stopped when the team saw Helena draw up her rifle and flashlight toward the far corner of the chamber. Rubio also focused his Glock in the same direction.

Paul took a step forward. "Helena? What's going on? What is it?"

She was unwavering in her stance but shaking a bit. Paul could see it in her hand.

"There's something in here with us," she whispered.

"Don't be daft, dearie. We're the only ones to be down here in ages," said Mav.

Paul turned to Rubio. "You saw it too?" The hacker shrugged his shoulders. "Not sure what I saw, but it was a shadow."

"You idiot," Mav chided him. "We're all casting shadows. See?" He pointed to their shadows on the gold.

Helena became defensive. "It was farther back in the room, asshole! I saw it move."

Everyone turned their flashlight to the other end of the chamber—and saw nothing but a solid brick wall with patches of dirt and piles of wood scrap from old chests.

Paul examined her closely. "So it's haunted; so what? There's nothing here; there's no other way down here."

Or is there? thought Don.

Amanda had learned all that she could of the man called Hugues de Lamonthe. His was a bitter tale told by others from outsiders' standpoints, but it was a different than the man's personal journals. Amanda was able to make out some of the old French, written in slanted script. The diagrams were just as revealing. Human anatomy mixed with demonic names and symbols was enough to make her want to run miles away from it all, but it was Lamonthe's plans for a specific ritual that caught her attention. She lost her focus as she felt the tickle of something crawling on her neck; she thought a spider, but it was all in her head. The cobwebs made her feel uncomfortable. Amanda always had been taunted for her fear of arachnids.

Fang was eerily quiet standing behind her, watching. He lit a cigarette and supported himself on a rickety iron table near the doorway.

According to Lamonthe's last journal, he had practiced in private with black rituals. Lady Lamonthe was ill from disease. Once she died, he went crazy and wrote of his ever-growing paranoia. The captain within his command threw accusations of his being ill fit and possessing poor judgment when it came to imprisoning enemy soldiers. Lamonthe also noted his plea to Satan himself, and the lengths to which he was willing to go to bring his wife back from the dead. He wrote about a dream he'd had from the devil and a voice that told him he needed to spill the blood of four priests. The priest's blood on the gold itself represented his greed. After the right markings were made with blood of the priests, his wife's body was to be set aflame. In order for the dark forces to birth life into her, a sacrificial dagger had to pierce his own heart as his body fell into the flames. He too would be reborn with a new heart, as his old was weak.

Amanda knew just how crazy it was, but from Lamonthe's previous practices, a lot was possible. She read how Lamonthe used the dark arts to gaze into the plans of an English invasion. Satan's help enabled Lamonthe to match English technology with the longbows, trained archers, and complex battle tactics. It was this demonstration of advancement that kept the people in line.

Amanda turned to the next pages, but they were empty. The last entry was November 17, 1347. What had happened? She was stuck in a whirlpool of possible conclusions. Different sources pointed out that Lamonthe never made it through the ritual, that he was killed by his own men and left to rot in the castle somewhere. Others say that he was pulled from his room at night and dropped into town to be torn apart by dozens of angry citizens. Another possible theory was an escape plan that Lamonthe knew about—and only him. She'd found it in another hand-drawn map but was unsure if she would share it with Paul. She folded it up and put it in her pocket.

As she thought for a moment longer, she heard a startling shuffle from above her. It was a slight noise in the total silence. She looked up at a black book that was nudged two inches from its place on the shelf. Its condition was strikingly pristine, almost as if it was brand new. Amanda felt cold, and she breathed on her hands, trying to warm them. She'd just glanced at her watch—it was six thirty—when she was frightened by a loud bang that echoed from the catacombs. She almost fell backward onto the table.

"What the hell was that?" Fang then got the call from Paul that they were blowing through another wall. Fang grunted and said casually in his Russian accent, "Don't worry about it, and hurry the hell up with that shit; I want to see what's going on."

Amanda quickly grabbed the new looking book with red trim around the edges. A grim-looking beastly icon was on the leather cover. She opened the book and saw vivid paintings of monsters piling atop each other in huge masses. The pages were smooth lambskin, and the artwork was detailed. One of the pages revealed black hairy beasts dragging naked people down into fiery crevasses. Some were even being eaten alive. The next page made Amanda drop the book, as she could not stomach it anymore.

Fang was diverted by a sudden noise coming from the wine cellar. He raised his UMP submachine gun with the light from it piercing the blackness. "Who's there?" He glanced over at Amanda quickly with his good eye. "You stay there."

She watched as Fang faded past the entrance. The sound was very faint, like a rat scuttling about the floor. To her left in the room she saw a wardrobe against the wall; inside was a black hooded robe. She felt her palms sweat, even though it was frigid in the room. Her flashlight was pointed at the moth-eaten fabric of the robe. She didn't know why, but she was drawn to it and found herself walking closer to it. Terrified but curious she was. The robe had strange symbols on the chest piece that hung over the shoulders. She had reached out to feel the embossed emblems made from leather that had been sewn onto the front of the robe. When the sleeve of the robe reached toward her head. A gray stony hand protruded from the end of the sleeve and grabbed the back of Amanda's neck with a grip so fierce she could not pull away. Her scream was stifled in her throat when her mind left her, and all she could see was light.

The warmth of flame. She had been cold a minute ago, but now hot air passed through her, and she saw flames dance on what looked like a golden sea. She heard the sounds of men yelling and laughing. In the flames was a pale-faced man with a trimmed black beard. He wore a black robe and stood on the pile of gold coins with his arms spread. In one hand he held a dagger. At his feet was a woman in a white dress. She looked beautiful but pale and lifeless. Her dress was being consumed by the fire. Her flesh was melting away. The imagery raged in Amanda's head. The man in the black robe took a crossbow bolt to the chest from a group of soldiers standing ten feet away. They began to retreat through a door as the man in the black robe shouted something as the flames licked his body. He was screaming frantically before the last bit of air drained from him. The faces of the retreating soldiers leaving the chamber showed they were sickened at the sight. Amanda knew it was Lamonthe. He fell to his knees with a bolt in his chest. Blood was all around him, glistening on the gold and silver.

Then it was all over. The scene blurred from her vision as darkness resumed, and she found herself on the stony floor. Amanda had heard about the psychics seeing visions of certain things of the past, but how had she been able to see something so clearly and frighteningly real, without any supernatural ability?

The robe in the wardrobe actually was not there at all. Just an empty black space.

"I think we've had enough games for now," said Fang, shining a light down on her. "Get up."

To his surprise, she rose up frantically and clutched his giant arms. "Radio your boss right now! Tell him not to touch that gold! Please—tell him to get out of that chamber."

The command seemed irrational. Fang wasn't sure how to interpret it. "What? You crazy?"

Amanda did not ask again but reached for the radio on his shoulder strap. She was only able to press the button and squeak a word before Fang threw her back into the table. He was so strong he seemed to effortlessly push her with one arm as she tried again.

"Stop! You have to tell them!" The second push into the edge of the table knocked over a few trinkets, skulls, and other alchemy-related items. One of them was a glass jar she'd noticed earlier, full of a white powder, most likely used for Lamonthe's studies. She fell on her rear with the tabletop just above her head. She heard the jar rolling toward the edge of the table and stopping.

Fang grinned, twisting the wicked scar around the curves of his cheek as he leaned over close to Amanda. "Ha ... you a silly girl. Got your head wrapped up in—"

Crack!

Amanda had reached up with both hands around the large glass jar. She then slammed it over Fang's head, breaking it. The sulfuric powder escaped into the air. The impact was enough to stun him, and she grabbed the top of his head, pushing it down to meet her knee with his face. This time he staggered backward onto the floor. Amanda had observed his combat knife in a sheath on his right shoulder strap. She pulled that out and ran with it, directing her flashlight toward the catacombs. There were several things she knew she could have done. Her opportunity to kill Fang with that knife and run up the stairs, back through the main hall, into the courtyard, and out the gates had been clear and was what anyone would have done. However, she didn't have the stomach to kill a man with a knife. She grabbed it for what was about to come. She knew Don, an innocent man, was still with them, and they had to be warned because she knew that what was coming was real, just like that vision. If they could listen to her just this once, she could stop it.

All she could do was scream as loudly as she could. "Don't touch it! *Stop! Stop!*" Amanda ran as if she were running for her life, but she was too selfless to run for her own life. She ran because there was a devil lurking in the castle, ready to awaken. If there was a devil, and if there was a deal with a dead man, it would not matter if that man was dead. The devil would see his plan though. *Studies of cults have revealed the forces of this, time and again,* she thought. Her screams echoed through the darkened halls until Paul Galley heard them.

"It's that historian bitch," said Jill. "What's gotten into her?"

Paul thought, *What could be the meaning of the distress?* He shrugged it off and motioned for Helena to grab her. "Go see what the fuck is going on, and bring her back here. I don't want her storming in here with a gun."

Jill laughed at the thought. "You think schoolgirl overpowered Fang and took his shoota?"

Paul grunted and turned back to the gold melted to the floor from the heat of flames that had engulfed the room centuries earlier. He heard Amanda's words billowing down the corridors of the gloomy halls: "Stop! Don't touch the gold!"

Rubio glanced at his watch and threw the duffel bags to the floor. "We have less than ten minutes before the guards' shift changes. We need to pack up," he said.

Paul was second-guessing himself but knew in his core that he had not come all that way for nothing. Amanda was a stupid, desperate hostage who was trying to confuse him and his team. "The pick!" he demanded.

Alonzo tossed him the pick ax. Paul felt nervous about something he couldn't describe. *What happened to my optimism?* He realized he'd awkwardly fallen from that zenith while listening to Amanda's warnings. Now there was a knot in his gut. He fought it. Pick ax firmly in his hand, Paul made the choice for wealth and gold that would be more than everything he could have imagined. The first swing was easy, but the point fell like a burden. The pick cracking off a piece of gold sent the first ripple of cold through his heart. Paul never had felt so numb about an action, especially when it came to stealing from an old tomb.

The room fell silent—and so did Amanda, who had stopped her frantic screaming. A low hum vibrated the wall around them, as if bees were swarming behind the stones. The pick felt like lead, too heavy for Paul to lift again, as he stared up at the skeletons chained to the supports. A bead of sweat crept down his cheek.

Helena had tackled Amanda to the floor and pinned her knife hand to the cold mud, where a puddle formed from the moist ceiling of the catacombs.

Amanda struggled, and shouted at Helena. "You don't know what you're doing! Stop!"

Helena slapped Amanda across the face so hard it took a moment for Amanda to recover.

"*Silencio!*" Helena snarled. "I don't give a damn about your little storybooks. We are taking what we came for! This castle is just another job, and so are you."

Amanda felt the faint vibrating as well and the sound of forces within the walls—the sound of bees but more deep and disruptive. Helena loosened her grip on Amanda. She slowly stood up as the cut stones within the dark warped in such a way that she thought she was delusional. Helena shook her head and felt the wall with her hand.

Amanda observed it to be normal, but there were strange, dark shadows swirling above her and an unusual echo that did not sound like it was a living person that pierced the silence. Amanda had to break it to them quickly. She hoped they would believe her. "The gold, dammit! It's cursed," she said, as the flooded part of the hall rippled. A smell more sickening than when they first entered seeped into the air. Amanda slowly got to her feet but did not bother running, as she was still examining the situation. In the chamber, the floor became covered by a thick blanket of fog. The roots and vines retreated back into the cracks of the stone and earth.

The team slowly backed away toward the entrance of the chamber, not saying a word. The vibrations and noise grew more violent.

"Why are the roots retracting?" said Mav.

"That noise—what's going on?" added Jill.

Distant unintelligible and distorted voices came in and out. The sounds seemed to travel in midair but the group could not pinpoint the source. The team shone their lights everywhere, but nothing was in the darkened room except the gold—and the gold was beginning to move. A small lump began to form near the center. It looked like it was melting but there was no heat.

"How is that possible?" Paul asked as the lump grew into what looked like a human shape and extended an arm, as gold dripped from the figure like melted cheese. The heat was now apparent as steam rose from the dripping gold and sizzled as it hit the cool floor. Other parts of the gold form started to boil. The bones of the two skeletons sunk into the yellow soup that was spreading farther out over the chamber floor. Paul's heart dropped to his gut as the arm pointed at them. The team was frozen.

They all were itching to run but had to register what this phenomenon was all about.

Their lights lost power, and the darkness in the room consumed them in a torrent of fear.

"We need to go now," Don urged.

"Shit!" Jill spat out as she slapped her light attachment. Alonzo was breathing heavily. Paul knew the temperature had dropped lower that it had been previously, but could feel intense heat as if they were inside an oven. Clicks sounded as everyone struggled to turn the lights back on.

Rubio's laptop also flickered out completely. "There's some electronic disturbance!" he cried, going for a spare battery. They heard another kind of breathing interspersed with the crew's curses—breathing like a beast would make through its gaping nostrils.

"He-e-y-y! Guys! I'm here!" shouted Helena. Her voice sounded strained as she slapped her flashlight.

"Damn light!" The light flickered on for a few brief seconds and revealed that the room, which had been empty, now was full of black figures that surrounded the team. The figures were hunched over and had disfigured limbs and monstrous faces, and they stood no more than five feet away.

The one next to Jill made an unbearable roar, showing its lines of two-inch-long jagged teeth in its foaming jaws. Don felt a bone-crushing grasp on his left shoulder and an unsettling hiss behind him. The light flickered off, and hellish screams filled the room, mixed with human screams. Paul couldn't see anything, but he knew where to go, and that was straight back out the way he'd come in.

7

Alonzo instinctively fired the first shots into what looked like black spaghetti noodles dancing where the lights hit briefly. "Run for the door! Get out!" The room lit up as Alonzo and Mav opened fire on the things that were now scattering everywhere like roaches. One moment they were all grouped together, and in the next moment, the sluggish-looking but fast-moving goblins were crawling up the walls and across the ceiling. Jill struggled with one that had grabbed her. Bursts from her Uzi illuminated the thing's bony body and the black holes she put through it.

"Help!" Don cried. He felt claws similar to an eagle's talons hooked into his shoulder, with a painful scraping on the back of his head. Paul fired a few shots before he stumbled into Rubio, who seem to be confused. Paul shoved him in the right direction. The shouting continued between Helena, Mav, and Jill, who was clutching her bloody arm when the next flicker of light showed the chaos in the chamber. Paul lit a flare and left it on the floor, which gave them enough light to see what was going on. He saw that Jill, Alonzo, and Mav were still inside, shooting at what seemed to be impossible targets, scurrying all over and leaping from above to deliver an attack with gnashing teeth and claws that extended like a bear's.

Don caught a lucky break as he used a stone to bash the beast's foot next to him. He couldn't reach the thing on his back but seemed to hurt it enough that the beast released him. *Or has it just decided to feast on someone else?* Don wondered. The red light from the flare made the beasts look even more hellish, with slits for their eyes and odd folds over their faces. Paul could not see much, and had to keep himself from running into the wall .

"Get the fuck out now!" The voice was Mav's. The noise was unbearable, with the roars and gunfire in a closed environment; it was a wonder that any of them could hear anything. Jill made it out, then Mav, dragging Alonzo, who had one clinging to him.

Don scrambled out and kept running, with Jill following suit. The little demon was clawing frantically at Alonzo's chest. He struggled to keep his face away while he repeatedly stabbed it with a Bowie knife. Paul watched in awe as he tried to steady his handgun on the thing. A shot rang out, and the thing's head exploded in a blob of blackish ink. Alonzo got up quickly and realized he was fine. The monster had shredded only his bulletproof vest. Paul grabbed Alonzo's arm and pushed him forward.

The team did not stop as the little demons began crawling out through the chamber door as well. Their scratches were tearing up the stone, leaving marks that Don would never forget, marks made on his consciousness as he mustered the strength to sprint back into the dark catacombs. He felt Rubio behind him, pushing past him. Blood trickled down Don's head and the back of his neck.

He did not dare inspect his wounds, as he was too focused on clinging onto the surrounding walls so he would not run into the beasts in the blackness. He then ran into one of the women and was met with a deep scream of panic and an arm flailing at him. He grabbed both her arms. Another flare was lit, and he saw it was Amanda, her eyes wide with terror and a knife in her hand.

"It's me, Don! We're leaving now! You're okay?"

Amanda could only nod, gazing into him. He turned her around, and they quickly caught up with Rubio, Paul, and Helena. In the light, they could see a few crawling over them and disappearing, making little clicking noises. Jill and Alonzo were not too far behind, yelling for everyone else to wait for them. The thought of being left behind in this place was unimaginable. Don wanted to sprint, but Amanda was trudging through one of the puddles they'd passed earlier. The last flare was beginning to fade as they approached the last bend in the catacombs. Another scream up ahead sounded like Helena and then more gun shots. Amanda managed to get her flashlight working and caught a glimpse of something else moving out of the pockets where the dead were put in the catacombs. Don did not stop to see what it was, but Amanda couldn't help but notice arms and hands. Pale white figures were growing from the spaces in the walls. Then it was heads and tails or tentacles flailing around.

Amanda sped up as another noise made her skin crawl. She heard a rattling sound like a snake and then a distorted whisper, similar to somebody talking into a revolving fan. Her beam of light finally caught the corners of the racks in the wine cellar. Footsteps smacked against the floor behind them. It was everyone else who lagged behind. The catacombs echoed with noises not from this world. The sunlight spilling down the stairs that led out of the cellar never looked so great to Don. Paul stopped near the torture chamber and shouted for Fang. His light pierced the room and the evil study room, revealing nothing.

"Where's Fang?" yelled Paul, staring at Amanda.

"I last saw him in there."

Paul looked furious but had no time to deal with Fang's disappearance. The shuffling and screeching from the catacombs grew louder. Fang never came out. Paul stopped Mav and told him to help with the wooden wine rack.

"What the hell? We need to leave!" shouted Mav.

"We'll block that stairwell," Paul said. "Help me quick!"

Don even helped to clear the full wine barrels off to make the rack lighter. The two were the last ones up the steps, trying to squeeze the rickety rack between the narrow walls.

"C'mon, pull!" The two of them were trying to get the oddly shaped rack wedged into the entrance when a heavy creature slammed into the other side, breaking off one side panel of the shelf and sending Mav flying backward. He lifted his shotgun while still on his back and emptied his last two rounds into the snarling beast. The second shot didn't kill it but scared it off. Alonzo and Rubio came in to help pull the shelf further in. The broken-off side seemed to wedge a little better into the wall. Helena was slouched over, wiping the sweat from her head. Alonzo was panting as he paced backed and forth. The other beasts that scurried close to the shelf were shot instantly.

"We can't stop here. Keep moving!" Paul pulled Mav up and pushed him forward. The group shuffled toward the door but noticed something odd with the walls. The walls were *moving*.

"The mess hall! Through there—it will be faster!" shouted Amanda over the growing screeching. Paul did not argue and charged the door. When it wouldn't open, he tried kicking it open. "Locked!" The door moved only three inches before being snagged by a chain and padlock.

Jill produced a backup 357 revolver from her jacket pocket and shot the padlock off the chain. The door flew open, and everyone poured in except for Helena, who stood fixed on a black material seeping in through the crevasses of the cobbled floor. She was in complete shock at the phenomenon and pointed as the black jelly defied gravity. It was molding into another strange figure.

"They're coming through …" Rubio stepped back to pull Jill through the doorway. Jill shut the door soon after. Don grabbed a maintenance light and wedged the stand at an angle that put the top just under the knob latch. The door then jolted from something slamming into it on the other side.

"What the fuck is going? What the fuck are those—" Jill's voice was brought to a deafening scream, and the group noticed her face was filled with aguish. Don was stunned to see a hand with black talons—so grotesque in the way they protruded from the fingers—digging into Jill's foot. Another unusual black claw, grown from the palm of the hand, also was tearing through her shoe. The demonic hand was forming slowly up from the stone floor like sweat leaving pores. Jill unloaded five shots into the slimy black claw. The shots severed it at the wrist, but the hooked claws still latched to her foot. The group was in disarray now, with Mav and Alonzo holding the door; Helena staring in shock at the hand; and Rubio watching ahead, with his weapon shaking in his sweaty hands. Paul was trying to pry the claw off Jill's foot. Her frantic curses did not help his focus. The skin on the black hand was moving like a blanket of worms. Don ran ahead but was halted by Rubio's shooting just over his head.

"Don't make me, asshole!" Rubio snarled.

Don froze and waited silently. Amanda's responsiveness was more ardent now. Her senses were alert. Survival was paramount. Amid the repetitious scratches at the door and the random screams from within the other rooms, she heard the rattling of chains coming from the winding hall to the right. The windows in the hall showed no outside light. It was night now, but luckily the automatic lights installed by LPS kicked on. The lights were dim, and flickered from time to time. The chains grew loud, and they witnessed the unexplained once again.

"Look out!" Amanda's warning was slurred due to her shattering scream, but Helena saw it too and ducked. A chain extending over twenty feet, with a wicked hook at the end, was moving on its own and lashed out at Helena. The hook bounced off the opposite wall while another took the tall woman by surprise. Chains were rattling. A second hook snaking over the floor wound up and buried its point directly through Helena's Achilles tendon. She winced in pain. In less than a second, the chain pulled her viciously from the back. She collapsed onto her face, with a crunch that was her nose breaking on impact with the floor. A bloody spot remained as she yelped and gagged from the knot in her gut.

Jill shouted, "Helena!" Paul leaped forward to grab her hands but was too late, as the chain and hook dragged Helena with alarming speed toward the window end of the hall. Helena shouted at the top of her lungs as her fingernails bit into the stone floor, trying to postpone her fate around the corner.

The other chain wiggled and caught Amanda off guard as the hook came about and wrapped around her ankles. The hook latching onto the chain created a loop that closed instantly around her legs. Amanda had never known such terror. Being kidnapped and thrown into a van seemed like a walk in the park compared to something as nightmarish as this. She knew how Helena felt, as Amanda could not let out a scream. Her diaphragm felt as though it tightened up as the chain tugged at her, and she fell on her back.

"Amanda!" Don shouted. He was quicker than Paul and reached for her hands. Amanda stared at Helena, clinging to the corner of the hall. Half of her face was covered in blood, and her teeth were locked together as she tried with the last bit of her strength to separate herself from the hook—and then another hook flew out and dug into her shoulder, ripping her from the corner. As her head flew back, her eyes were like saucers and her mouth was wide open with no sound. She disappeared, and everyone watched in horror at the spray of blood showering the opposite wall and window. The sound that followed was a mixture of a wood chipper or mechanized device and a creature gobbling raw meat. Amanda twisted over onto her belly, still clinging to Don's arms.

"Please help me! Please!"

Alonzo had come to his senses and raced over to fire a volley of rifle rounds at the chains, but it did nothing.

"Break them!" exclaimed Don. The tug-of-war was excruciating. Whatever was pulling had the strength of five men. Alonzo hit the chain with the pick ax several times, but it was stronger than any other man-made chain. Amanda had processed that as the material itself was so hot, it was burning through her slacks. She then realized that they would lose in terms of strength, so she wiggled her feet as much as she could. The ends of the pants were melted in a way that made the fabric weak to a point of tearing. It was the acrylic fabric that burned into a goopy black tar. It hurt like candle wax but the chain was sliding. Don became fatigued but Alonzo had grabbed her just as the sudden force whipped Amanda around the corner of the hall. Her back was sliding in a layer of Helena's blood. It had pulled Alonzo off his feet, and he came crashing down to the floor with her. Quickly, she anchored herself to a fixed statue of plated knight armor. She stole a glance down at the thing that was dragging her to her doom.

The monster was black with prickly hair all over it. She did not see legs, but there were two arms with the girth of basketballs and long claws tearing away at the stone like it was cheese. The beast's eyes could not be seen but its sheer size matched that of a truck, taking up the whole width of the hall. The grinding sound was not teeth or jaws but a series of four rapidly spinning rollers with rusted, bloody blades covering each roller. Like an industrial printer the rollers were offset. It was half mechanized and half flesh. The metal rim that connected the machine was staked down, pinning the device to the head of the fleshy beast. There was no head, but it had a large mouth that was a human blender. There was a large hole just above where the chain was fed through. Amanda felt Don tugging at the chain loop around her ankles. He winced with pain as the chain was burning his hands, but her feet eventually slipped out from her shoes and burned pants. The chain recoiled and danced around. Amanda was free and more relieved than ever. They did not hesitate to get up and sprint toward the mess hall exit.

The guard's hall had a table with chairs in the middle. Medieval displays, such as the food they ate and wine goblets, were arranged in an ornate manner until Mav and Jill tossed it over as a temporary blockade for anything that might be chasing them.

Paul stopped when he reached two doors, one on either side of him, and a set of stairs on the left. "Which way?"

Amanda pointed to the right. The door was already open, and they found themselves in the foyer behind the chapel, the same hall overlooking the courtyard with the statue to the right of them. The cold breeze through the stone struts chilled their sweat, making them feel colder, but was good all the same. More of the tiny fast creatures were spawning, much more quickly than they had been, from out of the cobblestone. Black tar-like figures slithering into demons were forming on the main tower wall. The team ran in through the cathedral back door.

Finally inside the cathedral, Amanda had to bar the

door shut with the wooden block that prevented the door from swinging inwards.

"Does this door have another lock?" Paul asked.

"It's usually meant to be open," Amanda answered.

Don noticed Alonzo on his knees, praying at the altar steps. Jill rested on the nearest bench to tend to her ankle.

"We're not out of here yet! Check the gate!" yelled Paul.

"It's past the new shift change. They might be waiting outside," Rubio reminded him.

"Then we'll gun them down. I'm not going to be eaten alive." Paul reloaded a fresh mag and rushed ahead through the main colossal doors they had passed through earlier. The steps were illuminated by lights built into the side guard walls. The sight of it hit Paul harder than everyone else, but Don also saw the gravity of their situation as they looked directly at a closed wrought-iron gate. Paul seethed with anger. Amanda headed to the right stairway, leading to the corner tower.

"Where the fuck you goin'?" said Jill.

"Find out about the gate," Amanda answered. "Where else am I going to go?"

Jill cursed and followed behind to investigate. The tower was dark inside but Amanda knew where to go.

"The old gate controls are for display purposes only, but there is an electrical power switch hooked up to hydraulics that lower and raise the gate. See?"

Jill shined her light on the floor where a panel was open just next to the old crank wheel that required sheer manpower centuries ago. Jill's radio crackled.

"Jill, you see about the gate?" It was Paul.

"It's been opened, and the switch has been messed with." Jill then picked up on something else just a few feet ahead.

"Getting something else … blood on the floor." Her light followed the red path to a dead animal. Jill and Amanda both jumped back but realized it was dead. Its pelt was tainted with its blood.

"A fucking wolf?" said Jill.

Amanda nearly fainted as rough hands gripped her shoulders from behind. She screamed and lunged forward to get free of the man who stumbled down to the floor. Jill focused her Uzi on him as he crawled a few inches and looked up. She could see it was another LPS guard, dressed in the black uniform, with a gun in his hand. Jill put her foot on the gun and kicked it aside but noticed it was empty—the chamber was open.

He looked up at them desperately and uttered something they could not understand. He rolled over on his side, revealing a torn shirt and a belly that was badly gashed. A chunk was missing from his left leg.

"He needs help!" cried Amanda, kneeling down.

Jill lowered her weapon. "He's already dead." The man died shortly after Jill had called it. Amanda checked his pulse; she assumed the wolf had killed him.

Jill's radio received more chilling news from Mav. *"Yeah, there's a few wolf carcasses lying around down here. What the hell, man?"*

Paul came on, sounding more aggressive as he barked at Jill. *"You find the fucking switch? I would like to get out of here sometime today!"*

Jill swallowed back her anger. "You bloody bastard, just thinking about yourself. What about Fang?"

Paul didn't respond. Jill opened the door that led outside on the battlement, directly over the entrance, to speak to him directly.

"You fucked us on this whole job! I didn't sign up for this mad shit!" she shouted.

Paul glared at her and pointed a finger. "You listen. Fang is dead. Nothing could have survived in there—"

Jill cut him off. "You let Helena die! What the fuck was that thing?"

Rubio withdrew his computer. He quickly discovered a new way to bypass the gate switch wirelessly while they argued. Despite the chaos and the groans of the ungodly things from inside, he managed to concentrate and found the remote switch himself. "I got the doors. We're home free," he said. The electrical power of the hydraulics hummed as the gate rose upward.

Amanda did not like this. *Am I really that much smarter than they are?* she thought, and then she shouted, *"No! What are you doing?"* She ran outside where Jill stood. "Close the damn gate! Fuck! What are you thinking?"

No one spoke as they waited for the gate to clear enough for them to leave. Amanda rushed back inside to the manual switch and flipped it to LOWER once again.

Paul noticed the gate begin to lower when it was four feet off the ground. He felt an urge to go up and put a bullet in Amanda's head but stopped himself when the growling from the dark grew louder. They all backed away from the gate as two wolves, with furious yellow eyes and jaws gaping open to bite flesh, managed to squeeze under it.

Quickly, Alonzo shot a burst at the first one and hit its hind end; the animal tackled Paul to the ground. It's growling was a horrific sound that demoralized Paul as he struggled to keep its gnashing teeth from his face. Don watched, hoping the wolf would succeed, but he kept a sharp eye on the other wolf, which changed course quickly and lashed out at Mav.

"Aww! Shit!" Mav cried. The beast clamped its jaws around Mav's arm but let go as he swung the shotgun around to put a slug in its side. A slight whimper was heard as its flailing body fell to the cobblestones. The wolf atop Paul was killed with a precise shot to the back of its head. Paul could feel the tension of its muscles loosen, and he tossed it over.

8

ill stood over him on the wall with a smoking revolver barrel. There were no words between them, but Paul realized his debt to her and the crew for dragging them into this. Everyone yet again fell into the pit of fear and worry as the outside gate was crowded with white-gray wolves, growling and howling at them through the grid-like iron gate. Rubio took aim, but Paul stopped him.

"Don't bother; there are dozens of them."

Their beams of LED lights revealed hundreds of the beasts blanketing the area around their van—patches of black, gray, and white, with yellow eyes glinting at them. Jill, scared and speechless, saw them as well.

"Our only way out is through that?" said Don, not expecting an answer. "I'm sorry, Sarah." His words were to himself as he thought about the wife and child he might never see again.

Paul looked back at Rubio. "Check the other sides of the castle."

Rubio's results were heart-wrenching as well. The night vision revealed even more wolves roaming the outside walls. Paul's expression was drained of life.

Amanda and Jill now were at ground level.

"Why would they all gather here?" Don asked Amanda.

"I don't understand. There never have been this many in one place," she answered.

Jill took one cold glance at her. "You got some explaining to do."

Inside the cathedral, the bulbs in the wall sockets were on but the room was still dim. Mav lit the candles in their holders that were placed alongside the aisles and benches. Alonzo was gripping his crucifix with his eyes shut, chanting prayers in Spanish. Mav threw down his weapon and kicked over a few boxes of ornaments, breaking the contents.

"Fuck! We got those out there and these fucking things in here. I either had a black-out or … or … I'm sitting on a park bench somewhere, overdosed on fucking drugs." Mav grabbed Amanda's face violently, demanding a response. "You vile little bitch! What just happened?"

Paul had to pull him away and pushed him down on the nearest bench. "Calm your ass down. We have to keep it low. Those things are just outside," said Paul.

"Why aren't they in here as well? They were popping up like weeds earlier," said Jill.

"This is a holy place, a place unfit for tortured or damned souls," suggested Alonzo.

"This whole castle is damned." Amanda's words shut them up, and they listened intently to her next words. "When you were tearing away at the vault chamber, I made a discovery on the history of this place, things I did not know before. The gold you saw in that chamber not only belonged to the man known as Hugues de Lamonthe but the devil."

Mav scoffed, "You shitting me? Fuck sake, now I've seen it all."

She sat down and drank from a water bottle Don handed her. Then she continued. "The gold was a part of a sacrificial ritual that was interrupted by Lamonthe's own men, who plotted to kill him because of his madness and lack of leadership. The ritual was to bring his wife back from the dead using the blood of four priests and the gold acquired from his lust for it. I know this sounds beyond this world, but believe me when I say that he made a vow that whoever might lay his hands on the gold would suffer the wrath of hell." Recounting it had nearly brought her back to that place in the study. "His men heard the curse over the flames that devoured Lamonthe and took heed. They sealed the entrance. It's why I was trying to stop you … God, you're so stupid. All of you should have listened."

Paul leaned against a stone support column with his arms crossed. "What happened to Fang?" Amanda had to lie for her sake. Her GI Joe stunt definitely would earn her a bullet.

"I snuck past him when he went to check out a noise. I swear it was the last time I saw him."

Mav rubbed the stubble on his cheekbone as he leaned in toward Paul. "She could be right, mate. There's also that other prick wandering around."

Don cut in. "Louis. His name is—"

"I know that cunt's name," Mav snarled, "and if he did anything to Fang—"

"They could be both dead," Paul interrupted. "Who knows? Fang was closer to the entrance when this all went down, so he could have gotten out first."

"The van is still there, along with the security guards' truck. What you saying? He managed to outrun wolves?" asked Jill. Her opinion rang logical.

Alonzo suddenly remembered the roadside surveillance set up from earlier. "Hey, what about the change in guard shifts? Did they come in?"

Rubio began typing in his Toughbook. Don answered, "They came in at six thirty on the dot, as always. They probably figured I was still busy or tried to get hold of me."

"Radio comms are blocked when underground. It's why we got nothing," said Rubio. He noticed the new guards coming in and the others leaving. Two stayed at the shack while two continued to roll on by. Rubio's eyes narrowed at Don, peering at him with intensity. "Think you might want to see this, Paul," said Rubio.

Don had a bad feeling about what the cameras had pulled up—something he kept from them that he should have said, now that the circumstances had altered. At 6:35 on the recording, a truck pulled into the utilities yard just outside the gate with two guards.

Paul was already furious. Don stood, not knowing how he was going to receive his punishment—or execution.

"That's the man I saw in the gate room," Jill said, "the same fucking bastard bleeding out." She referred to the slender guard who was on the recording and was the same who died from his wounds.

"Don, what have I told you?" said Paul.

"I told you everything, and I was certain that night shift did not do an inspection at that time; I meant it."

Paul came closer, ignoring his excuse. "Haven't I given you specific instructions to deliver information to me beforehand? I'm pretty sure I told *you to inform me*!" Paul stepped forward and kneed him in the gut. Don folded over, heaving as Paul slammed his Glock handle over the back of his head. Don fell to his knees as Amanda shouted at Paul to stop.

Paul stopped to collect himself for a moment and remembered. He withdrew his phone and flashed it up with one hand. "Oh, don't you worry about what might happen to you, Mr. Millar. I know of a certain way to get you to learn."

Don knew he was talking about his family. "*No-o-o!*" As he lunged forward, Paul defended with a move that redirected his attack, followed by a severe blow to the gut and a stinging kick to the side of the knee, causing Don to fall. Amanda was nearly in tears yet again, feeling afraid for the beaten man. Paul dialed and awaited the henchman he called the "Bogeyman" to pick up.

A moment went by, and the ringing stopped. Paul didn't wait for the Bogeyman to say hello; he immediately said two simple words: "Do it."

Don's face was red with fury, nearly foaming at the mouth as he tried to regain his breath. "I'm   gonna kill you!"

Paul did not mind the threat, but he was still waiting for a response from his man. The sounds on the other end of the phone were unusual. Concerned now, he repeated his instruction. Don knew something was off. Amanda bit her lip. "Hey, are you listening? Hello?" Paul heard whispering. He turned the phone volume up but still struggled to hear the raspy voices in the static.

Don watched as the tables turned. This time Paul was alarmed, and Don was relieved. The phone suddenly cracked with a high-pitch squeal. The sounds were a mesh of screams and laughing and then voices that were faint, as if nothing had happened. The phone was not on speaker but everyone in the room could hear the sounds of several entities finding their voices and invading every airway and signal. Paul's face was now engulfed with dread. Jill had not seen him so pale.

Don, on the other hand, took this opportunity. His family would be safe, and all he had to worry about now was his survival. He had a last-ditch method, however. With his hand near his shoe, he felt for it—the bone—but the reflection in the silver holy water font gave it away. In frustration, Paul pointed the barrel of his gun at Don's head, ready to finish him off. Paul's other plan was void, and he now had to take measures into his own hands.

"It's over, Millar."

Don pulled the broken-off shin bone from his shoe—small bone the size of a shiv that was broken to a sharp point. Don had smuggled it from the catacombs earlier. He rammed the point into Paul's left knee and at the same time pushed his gun hand aside, just as a shot went off. With his hand still on the shiv bone, Don plucked it back out and watched as Paul folded over, screaming. However, Don, in his panic, failed to rip Paul's gun away and did not take into account the rest of the crew scrambling for their own guns.

"*Run!*" Amanda screamed as she too took action, using the silver font as a bludgeoning object. She swung it at Jill's head, knocking her unconscious. Everyone else's shots zipped in Don's direction as he remained crouched between the benches and rolled behind the side support columns closest to the walls. Things happened so fast, but Don felt like it had slowed down, as every shot blast was counted. Mav noticed Amanda's stunt, and he went after her rather than going for the shotgun he'd tossed aside earlier. He dived as she retreated for the double doors.

"Ahhh!" Amanda cried. Mav's rough hand grabbed Amanda's ankles before she could get away. As she fell to the velvet carpet, she was reminded of that thing that had a hold on her only moments before. Don thought he felt a bullet pass through his side, but it was a piece of broken wood from the shots chipping off debris from the benches. In the midst of his heart pounding, Don noticed other gunshots popping off from the organ room in the far corner. Don rolled behind the first stone support pillar, shielding him from a burst of automatic fire. Once he knew the shots were diverted, he peeked around to see what was happening.

It was Louis—the other guard who'd managed to get away before this nightmare began. Armed with only his Glock, he strafed sideways into the church, landing a shot on Alonzo's right leg. Rubio decided to go for cover, ducking behind a pew.

"Louis, get down!" Don's warning came too late as the valiant guard was put down by a few well-placed shots by Rubio. Don decided to make his move and run down the side, keeping to the stone supports. Amanda happened across a toolbox near one of the benches with a screw driver on the top of the lid. She snagged it in time and bent over to plant the end through Mav's hand that had a hold on her foot. She grunted as she put her entire strength into the attack, but she managed to pierce his hand deeply enough that it came out his palm.

"Bitch!" Mav let go instantly, crying as he nursed his bleeding hand.

Amanda took to the door, with Don not too far ahead. She felt a few bullets zip by. At the other end, Louis bought them some time as he fired back from the floor near the podium. It turned the gang's attention back toward him, as they managed to run out safely through the front. Louis was not as lucky; Paul put a bullet in his head to ensure he stayed down. Paul was furious as he turned toward Jill, who was just beginning to get up, rubbing the back of her head. Mav was painfully sliding the screwdriver out of his hand as Alonzo made a cloth tourniquet for his leg. His hostages had bested him, but Paul knew they wouldn't survive, not with an army of darkness looming within the walls.

Don helped Amanda up the stairs leading into the corner tower. She felt a gnawing pain in her ankles that prevented her from running too fast. In addition to that, she was barefoot from escaping the clutches of the blender that ate Helena. Amanda knew where to go and directed Don to hang a left, away from the adjacent gate and along the top of the wall, toward the southeast end of the castle. They were not surprised that they were not pursued. Don, Louis, and Amanda had done a number on Paul's gang but it was not without sacrifice. Don would never forget about Louis and what he did. As they continued to run through the next tower, Amanda stopped to shut the heavy wooden steel-framed door, just as they got inside the tower.

"Why are we stopping?" asked Don. Amanda shattered open a display case using a nearby exhibit stand. The case held medieval weapons that the soldiers had used to guard Black Sun. She grabbed an old dagger and slid it in her belt. She tossed Don a rustic-looking battle ax. He caught it without asking. Amanda ripped a large studded shield from a display armor set and wedged it under the door handle.

"Just in case they come up here. Let's go." They continued down the wall through the brisk night air with a dense fog settling overhead. The noises were faint now but could still be heard farther in. Ahead were the top floor barracks in a rectangular-shaped building. Amanda and Don stopped just outside of the door, hesitant.

"Aren't you going to open it?" asked Don.

Amanda looked back, worried, and then she peeked down over the ledge to get a glimpse at the wolves roaming below. "I just ... I don't know what might be in there."

Don noticed she was shaking, and he grasped her shoulders. "Hey, hey." Looking into her sobbing eyes, he tried to do his best to encourage her. "It won't be long before the authorities show up. You did good back there. If there is anyone I would rely on, it's you, Cohen. It's cold out here, so let's take our chances. Keep it low—I don't know if these things can hear us."

She nodded and they entered the dark barracks. The inside was done up for the troops, with old beds and goose-feather pillows. Foot lockers were at the end of each bed. The center of the room had an old brazier and weapon rack. So far nothing stood out or made any sound. The room seemed safe. Amanda looked down the flight of stairs to the left, where the lower floor barracks were, and then looked at Don.

"Help me with this bed would you?" she asked. "I want to block this entry." They team-lifted one of the beds and tossed the wooden frame into the stairwell. She then looked over at the two doors in the opposite corner. "We need to block those as well. That one leads into the main castle."

Don pointed at the brazier. "This thing looks heavy enough. Help me with this." The iron brazier was so heavy they both had to push with their backs against it. Slowly they pushed it across the room and tipped it up and over, letting it fall on its broad side against the door. Nearly out of breath, they started looking for something else. Don decided to sacrifice his ax for the time being, and he wedged the head in the narrow gap near the floor.

"We'll just have to watch that one. You can get some rest first while I take watch," he said, sitting down on one of the beds.

Amanda didn't argue. She sat there collecting her thoughts. "I can't believe this. It's like a dream. Like something from the *Twilight Zone*."

Don smiled at that. "We got to have hope. It's real enough, what's going on, but we've already been through the worst of it," said Don.

"Have we?" Amanda's question was left unanswered as she lay down on her side. "Oh, and hey."

Don looked over at her. "Hmm?"

"Nice move on that asshole," she said.

Don laughed a little at the thought of it. He had never done anything genuinely heroic in his life, but that night he considered himself a hero who had saved himself from execution. Amanda had been in no actual trouble with Paul, but he noticed that she'd taken the risk to help him. "You're a damn brave woman," he said quietly.

Amanda didn't hear him, as she was already asleep.

An hour later in the cathedral, the crew, having patched themselves up, continued to rant at each other for their petty mistakes.

"Nice going for the girl, Mav. You had your shotgun right there," scolded Rubio.

Mav flipped him off.

"What about you, tosser?" Jill shouted at Rubio. "You didn't see that bitch clip me in the head with a bloody water stand?"

"Enough!" said Paul. "We got the guy who was armed. He could have taken any one of us out. For God's sake, look at Alonzo. The two are as good as dead with no weapons and in there with those mutants. To hell with them."

"Are we forgetting the bit about the phone being tied up? Jesus, Paul, what was that?" Jill asked.

"What did you think it was? This voodoo shit is scrambling signals."

"So what's the plan now? We just trapped in here or what?" asked Alonzo, wiping the sweat from his head.

The air was frigid, but the gunshot he suffered made him clammy.

"I had Rubio send a distress message to my contact. Should be sending a chopper to the roof since we can't go out there." Paul was still spooked over that phone call. He then looked to Rubio. "Have they gotten to your connection?"

"It showed the message was sent. Let's hope," said Rubio.

"Yeah? And when was that?" asked Jill.

"Not too long after those two decided to play hero."

Paul then turned to Rubio. "You got anything back on that?"

Rubio opened his Toughbook and noticed something was wrong with the screen. The light flickered and the resolution changed colors from neon blue to purple to red. Command prompts tried to populate but flashed off and on as Rubio tried typing them in. "What the hell? I think I'm being hacked. Something is wrong."

Jill narrowed her eyes at him. "I thought you said we were running on an untouchable LPS network? You think they caught on?"

"No way. We got valid clearances from Millar. We have total immunity, but this is something destructive. Disruptor, I'm guessing." Rubio froze as the next image took him by surprise. The screen remained vibrant red but displayed a little girl in an old dress standing in the middle of the screen. Her head bowed slightly as she stood in one of the rooms in the castle. An arched window just behind her was surrounded by stone.

"No …"

Paul looked concerned. "Rubio, mate, what's the deal?"

Rubio continued to gaze at the girl, who then looked up at him. His heart sank as she began to speak. The audio sounded scratched and distorted. Her French accent even sounded accurate to Rubio.

"You should really come home, brother. We're all waiting for you."

Rubio shook his head in disbelief. "No, there's no way."

Paul spoke even louder. "Rubio! What's the deal?"

Jill and Paul both rushed over to see the screen for themselves. The walls behind her were slowly fading to black, like a growing cancer.

"It's very scary down here, brother." Rubio grabbed at his hair, frustrated and confused.

"That's not her, Rubio," said Paul. The screen flickered to black and white and then back to red. This time it showed a man with a cloth in his mouth. He was a brute, with a thick neck and a scar over an artificial eye. The man on his knees in front of the girl was Fang. He looked at her, docile and unmoving, as if he was under a spell.

"Shit, it's Fang! He's alive!" yelled Jill.

Paul told her to shut up as the girl continued to speak her last chilling words.

"Welcome to hell, brother." Soon after, she reached over and slid a knife across Fang's throat. The crew watched as the big man's mouth gaped open, and he spit out blood that looked black on the red screen. His body fell forward, out of sight, as the girl morbidly began licking the blood off the blade.

That's when Paul slammed the screen down and

tossed the Toughbook off to the side. "Fuck me!" he said alarmed.

"She's in here! She's alive!" Rubio started to run for the door, but Jill and Alonzo caught him and restrained him.

"That was not your sister, Rubio! She's been dead for years, remember?" said Paul.

"Dammit, Rubio, stop! It's not her; it's a trick!" said Alonzo fighting to keep him calm.

Rubio stopped his frenzy and fell to the floor with his head down, weeping. The image was vivid and exactly like his little sister who had died when they were kids.

"So that wasn't really Fang then either?" asked Jill, breathing deeply.

Paul raged. "I don't know! Shit, I think these things got into all of our electronics. Fuck, I …" Paul fell to the nearest bench. "I don't even know if the message was sent."

"So we make for the roof anyway. Light some sort of fire," said Jill.

"And risk the next people who arrive being the authorities? What are we going to do when they ask about Don?" Paul demanded.

"Get in those dead guards' uniforms. We'll tell them that Millar is injured, and we can't move him," she suggested. "Then when they get out, we'll hold the pilot and tell him to fly out of here. We can get far away, back to the safe house in Spain."

Paul liked that idea, but he realized they had to get to the roof through more of those things. "We should leave at least three here in the church, where it's safe. They don't seem to want to come in here. Alonzo can't walk too well, and neither can I. Mav's hand is fucked. Rubio and Jill, you two would have to apprehend the chopper and then get the pilot to fly close to the wall so we can jump on from there without it even landing."

"Oh right, Paul! You think Rubio is in any condition? Look at him; he's fucking mental from seeing his dead sister."

Paul looked over at Rubio, who was staring into nothingness with a dull expression on his face.

"Fine, dammit. We'll go together."

Something strange happened just then. A deathly chill came across them as all the candles they had lit earlier went out. The room fell into total darkness, except for the pale moonlight easing through the stained-glass windows.

"No one panic; just stay alert," said Paul, trying to sound confident.

"What's this now?" whispered Jill. The candles in the stands along the walls lit up again from nothing. Not only did they light up, but flames ignited from the support pillar sconces and the iron gothic chandelier hanging from the high, vaulted ceiling. All thirteen candles lit up at once. The large room was twice as luminescent as it was before. "The candles—how …?"

"Don't even try to figure it. We're obviously in some serious shit we need to get out of—and fast," Paul said.

9

ang felt a little like it was home, back in the pit of the gulag, but this time there was a different odor. It was not mildew but more like burning and decay. In the east part of the castle, just outside of one of the rooms, a door creaked open. The inside hall was dim as the rough-faced Fang stepped out from one of the servants' rooms. He was hiding from the thing that he'd seen earlier in the wine cellar and now felt less threatened, especially with the wall sconces lit. The dark seemed cruel to him, reminding him of the prison he was locked up in back in Russia. Fang had been cornered by many monsters, only in the forms of men, but the thing he saw earlier was fast and immune to bullets.

Not knowing exactly where he was, he tried to get his bearings. After he ran from the sublevel, he went for the door in front of him just after the stairs, but a black figure drew him away, and he turned toward the servants' quarters. He remembered the screaming down the hall where they had come in, and he knew that way was dangerous. He figured that the rest were gone or dead by now. He looked to the right and saw more wooden doors that were already open, revealing the small rooms where residents of the castle had slept. He made a sharp right

110

and went down a different hall, going east into the castle. To the left was another long hallway with two doors on the left and two windows on the right that looked outside. Fang could see nothing but black in the glass as the light from inside was overwhelming. He heard the echoes of faint humming and distant voices throughout the cold halls, but he could see nothing. He kept telling himself they were not real.

A woman was singing a high note somewhere in one of the rooms, but the sound was inconsistent. Fang took one of the bronze candleholders from a cubby hole in the wall to better light his area. It felt like hours had passed before he reached the end of the hall. There were steps at the end that went up and a door on either side of him. Fang tried the one on his right, but it would not budge. He knew it led outside which is why he had to try to open it. He plowed into it with his shoulder, and on the second try, it cracked open a foot—and something from the outside quickly forced it shut again. The force was so strong it pushed Fang backward off his feet. His candles went out, and he was left in a dim hall with something outside keeping him in.

A girl's laughter crept through the air. Quickly, Fang got up and grabbed the next wall sconce in the hall and headed for the stairs. This time he was stopped by the creaking sound on his left. The door opened to another room, larger than most. Two large tile baths were in the center, and elaborate stone-carved pillars were on each corner with a grotesque scene of demons raping an angel in a frieze painting.

The large brazier in between the baths was lit as well

as the torches on the side walls, revealing all of it. The hall behind him was totally dark as he stood in the doorway. His legs were frozen as he contemplated this particular room. There was water in the baths, as if somebody had prepared it all. A ghastly breath exhaled behind him and blew out the flame to his torch. He turned around quickly and saw a white, ghostly face with a beak-like nose. The disfigured face had eyes that were absolute red with a large gaping mouth full of filed-down pointed teeth, like a shark's. The figure was hanging upside down from the high ceiling, with a moth-eaten hood over its head that seemed to droop upward defying gravity. Fang was like a statue and in total shock as this thing let out a bloodcurdling scream before it grabbed Fang's head with one lanky hand. With its other hand it dug its long pointed nails into Fang's good eye and dug out his eyeball from the socket.

Fang groped for his lost eye, crying in agony. The demon's other hand had its nails dug into his skull like meat hooks, keeping him from retreating while it popped his eye into its mouth as a snack. The beast released Fang's head and let him stumble backward blindly into the large bath. Fang kicked and shouted for help. The taste of his own blood in the water frightened him even more. He fought and reached around for the edge of the bath. He pulled his head out of the water as one hand cupped his eye socket. Just as he stood up to put a knee on the edge of the bath, the demon then teleported into the bath and rose up from the water to grab him.

"*Paul!*" His cry was ended when the beast opened Fang's throat with a long blade. Blood coated his chest and spilled down into the water. The demon disappeared like fog in the wind as the heavy man fell lifeless into the bath.

Mav searched his bag for a few flares to give to Jill for signaling their ride. Paul checked the two radios that had the best battery juice and tossed one to Alonzo.

"I know it might sound useless, but we have to hope the radios will still work." Paul looked at his watch. "It's almost 1:00 a.m. We have enough dark to make a scene with the flares. Hopefully they won't try to wiggle their way through the wolves, but I doubt it. We don't have much ammo, so be wise with what you shoot up. If you see Cohen or Millar, I do suggest using a few rounds to take them down."

Mav laughed. "They'd be stupid to come back here."

Alonzo handed Paul his assault rifle.   "H e r e , you need it more."

Paul looked at him, puzzled. "Why you giving up your weapon?"

"It's not bullets that will stop these things. You battle evil with faith." Alonzo meant what he said, but Mav scoffed.

"You think God would let something like this on earth? If I were you, I'd keep your shoota, mate."

Paul ignored that and told Alonzo to keep his weapon. He headed for the door with Jill.

When Paul opened the back door to the cathedral, the foulest stench seeped in—a mixture of burned flesh and rot. Jill gagged and shielded her face with the crook of her arm. Paul noticed the backside of the door was nearly shredded, apparently by something scratching at it. Black-looking paste that was like tar marked the stone floor to the outer corridor. The sconces and torches outside and within the courtyard were lit as well. The chipped statue of the hybrid winged angel-demon remained static under the light. The two inched out slowly, more alert than ever, with guns pointed outward.

Though it looked like something had happened, it was surprisingly quiet. Fog prevented them from seeing anything past the north arch support to the far left. Jill jumped at the sound of a long wolf howl.

"Relax," said Paul. His knee was throbbing, but he was determined to push on, even if he was slow. "You still remember where we're going from the blueprints, right?" he asked Jill.

"Yeah, through the door there." She pointed to the left where they had first gone in.

Paul rammed it, as it seemed stuck for some reason. The door flew open, and Jill rushed in. Her automatic Uzi scanned the great hall. Paul followed close behind and froze as Jill's face fixed on something farther into the lit room. Once he saw what she was looking at, all logic and courage left him. The black iron chandelier swayed slowly over the large table that held piles of unusual dead things, chopped up and raw. Flies buzzed over the red meat, and what looked like black eels danced around without heads on the soaked wood. Paul thought he was hallucinating at first but saw that Jill was experiencing the same.

At the table, feasting on the meat and random body parts, were people. To Paul's amazement, they were not actual people but things dressed in French garb from another era. Four men wore purple and black tunics with studded leather underneath and hard metal helmets. Three women with pale disfigured faces were dressed in noble blue gowns and women's hats. Their dress looked lavish, but their nature was obscene as they chewed vigorously on pieces of flesh. An ax blade was firmly planted in the corner with a chunk of meat bleeding next to it. They were like a table full of barbarians but totally unaware of everything going on around them. Their hands dug into what looked like an intestine and forced it down they're mouths. Paul couldn't make out most of their faces as they chowed down.

He noticed Jill was breathing excessively and loudly. Paul put his finger to his lips to tell her to stay calm and signaled toward the door to the kitchen that led to the stairs to the tower.

Slowly and quietly, they slid to the right, as far away from the gruesome smorgasbord as possible, keeping their eyes on the beasts the entire time. Their feet somehow carried them closer to the kitchen. As they passed by the stone support column, Paul felt relief at being in the darker part of the room. They approached the door even quicker, but the kitchen door burst open before them. Startled, Jill fell back into Paul. He caught her and regained his balance, with one hand on the rifle, holding it toward the giant figure in the doorway.

Monstrous as the figure was, Paul could not pull the trigger. He dared not to, as he considered Alonzo's words about bullets being useless. The figure was broad-shouldered and wearing a white long-sleeved shirt with gussets at the shoulders. It wore ragged leggings made of linen and a cook's apron with fresh blood splattered all over it. The thing was double Fang's size. In one hand it held a large butcher knife and in the other, a human head. The giant's muscular face was small, and it grunted down at them. The eyes were black voids under a thick brow line with no hair. The bottom part of its face was sewn up, with black thread over the mouth. The silent servant. Then out of nowhere, a voice crackled, and Paul's nerves tensed all the more.

A voice, sounding so coy and casual, echoed through the hall. "Guests, have you come for the feast?"

Paul turned and saw a man in the tall throne chair, though no one had been sitting there just a moment ago. Now there appeared a deformed man, wearing royal garb. He raised a golden chalice toward them. His eyes were black like the cook's, and his skin was pale with purple veins that made him seem dead. The rest of the table guests looked at them, eerily silent from their chairs, with blood dripping from their decaying zombie lips and jagged teeth. The thing at the head of the table grinned a wicked grin and started laughing. The sound was part human yet a bit demonic.

"You're just in time for the main course!" The giant undead cook threw the head at Jill, who dodged it and watched it roll on the floor, looking back up at her. The face was Helena's, with part of her jaw missing and eyes rolled back up into the head. Horrified, Jill could not do anything but look. Paul had to tackle her off to the side, just as the cook attacked with the butcher knife.

"Get up! Go for the stairs!" Paul helped her up and turned to unleash a burst of ten-millimeter rounds into the cook's chest. The bullet holes seemed to punch through the flesh but did not even get the giant to stop for a second. It groaned through its sealed mouth and started marching for them. Jill got to the other side of the room, where they had come in, and saw there was another set of stairs they hadn't seen before. The entrance was cluttered with maintenance tools and materials. Jill also unloaded a burst of rounds into the cook. Little black holes sprouted with tiny black leeches falling from them, as if the cook's body was filled with the creatures.

"That won't do!" Jill cried. "Help me with this."

Paul limped to her and started helping her clear a way to the stairs on the left side of the grand hall. Jill threw a folding ladder in the path of the cook, who was getting closer to them. The ladder landed on its side, blocking the short gap in the arched support columns. Paul also pushed over a stack of boxes loaded with supplies in the gap. The cook stumbled over the clutter and fell face first to the floor. Paul then helped Jill grab the corner of a large wooden crate and pulled it back.   It was heavy but they managed to get it far enough away from the wall to squeeze past it. Jill passed through first with ease, but Paul struggled through.

"C'mon, hurry!" she yelled.

Paul wiggled his way through, just before the cook's arm reached in, flailing the knife around in the gap. As they started up the long stretch of stony steps, they heard a crunching noise behind them and stopped to discover that the large wooden box had broken open, and the cook was forcing his way through. Paint cans and preserving chemicals spilled out over the floor. Some burst open, leaking everywhere.

"Paul, light a flare!"

Paul did not want to sacrifice a flare, but as the thing started for them, he quickly withdrew a flare, lit it, and tossed it at the busted cans of primer. The heat from the fire was intense, and the base of the steps was consumed in flame that licked up the sides of the cook. Paul and Jill had reached the top when they noticed the cook had kept walking up but was slowing down as its flesh was burning up. Tissue dripped down off the bones in big black clumps of tar. The blackened figure that was once the cook seem to be morphing into something else. An inhuman yelp and screeching noise stirred through the flaring black creature, with arms whipping in every direction.

Jill stood in shock as the once-giant cook transformed into an unexplainable thing with nine tentacle-like arms and bones that seemed to reanimate into jelly moving on its own.

"Jesus, Paul, what the fuck is that?"

Paul grabbed Jill's arm and pulled her into the next room, just as the black thing turned into slime and spread across the width of the stairwell, moaning. Smoke from the stairs filled the next room quickly, making it hard to breathe. They ventured into the library, with finished wood shelves that reached the ceiling. They scanned the room thoroughly before proceeding. Paul's footsteps caused the wood boards to creak. The wall sconce at the end of the hall was burning brightly, revealing another door. The rest of the library was too dark to see, but Jill jumped at the sound of shuffling. She emptied the last of her rounds into the dark, blindly.

Paul smacked her weapon downward, glaring at her. "Don't fire until you can get a shot!"

She was hyperventilating and shaking but nodded when Paul repeated himself. When he turned, the last bookshelf at the end fell over on him and blocked the hall leading out. Jill did not see what knocked it over, but she withdrew her pistol and shot in the direction, forgetting already what Paul had said. Jill's flashlight shone into the room as she was trying to figure out where the thing was that knocked over the bookshelf. Paul struggled, as it was solid oak and filled with books. He grunted as Jill started walking backward toward the stone wall. Paul felt as if the object had squeezed the air from his lungs. The force of the bookshelf was tremendous. It hadn't fallen on Paul; it had been thrown down on him, but as he regained a grasp on the floor to pull himself out, he felt his voice return. "Keep... keep ..."

Jill was in shock but her focus was targeted on the dark part of the room. Paul's voice was a fading, muddy sound that went unnoticed. Jill's hands, already cold and clammy, turned white from the gun metal pressing into her skin. Once her back hit the wall, she seemed to snap back to her senses. Just for a moment, her concentration swiveled back to Paul and his last words to her: *"Keep running!"*

The wall behind Jill's head morphed, and between the crevasses of the stone two clawlike hands reached through and dug into her face. She let out a cry Paul had never heard before. Jill was always the tough girl of the bunch, but this had broken her. The nails made a crescent-moon hook and were as sharp as eagle talons, scratching flesh from her cheeks. Paul froze as the torch above him in the wall went out, leaving him in near darkness. The firelight from the stairwell was the only bit of brightness that showed the black silhouettes of Jill and the two things trying to grab her. The black figures were like snake tails, dancing around Jill as she spent two more bullets on one of the tails but then was knocked down. On the floor, she flipped over on her back and emptied the rest of her clip at the ceiling.

A terrifying scream with the high point of an elk call was mixed with that of a woman's yelp. Paul realized the creature was hit but did not stop. Another black figure, which seemed to be the main body of the creature, came down from above and slammed Jill back into the floor. Paul could see the body of a snake and the torso of a human attached to it, with arms that were scythes. It wrestled with Jill but easily overpowered her in strength and was causing damage.

Jill was clobbered and stabbed by this thing as Paul struggled to reach for his pistol. Her screams faded as the sound turned into gurgles of blood. Paul had to see, so he tossed in a red glow stick. The subtle change disturbed the creature. Its coiled tail was as thick as a tree trunk. The weight rested on Jill as the upper part of the beast turned ninety degrees, facing Paul. It sprang forward, revealing itself in the glow of the light. The skin was an ash-white with breasts waggling side to side with its movements. There was a large gaping hole in the lower abdomen that gave no indication of organs. The hissing face quivered, and Paul saw gold metal horns atop its head. The face seemed more like a mask—elaborate and slightly primitive, similar to that of an African tribal mask with boar tusks for teeth. The gold horns grouped on the head and narrowed down to a curved plate going over the nose. The eye holes were squinted, surrounded by ash-white flesh.

After it made some unrecognizable curse in another language, it turned its attention upward and used its tail muscles to lift itself back into the rafters in the vaulted ceiling. Paul could not see up there but knew that's where they were slithering around. Jill's cries continued, piercing the cold air. Paul managed to get out from under the shelf and go for Jill, still wrapped in the end of the snake tail. Just as he dived to grab her she was lifted up by the tail and disappeared in the dark area of the ceiling. Her shouts ended when Paul could hear slight tearing, and what sounded like chomping. The torch light on the wall lit up on its own again. Paul caught a glimpse of a body coming down upon him and was forced to leap to the side just as it thudded the floor.

Jill was dead, but her body wiggled around like a worm, with her arms missing from her sockets and her lower legs cut off. Paul dared to look up, and droplets of blood showered his face. The tails of those sinister things wrapped tightly around the rafters, and the knife arms held the limbs up to their faces, making a meal of Jill's parts. Paul ran back over the shelf, grabbing his pistol in the process, and headed for the door he'd seen at the end of the hall. In the dim candlelight of the scribe study were shadowlike figures crowded around. Different entities began to populate the large room. Paul knew he had to get through that door, now that there was no alternate way to go. The dark human figures swaying side to side were advancing slowly, shuffling closer to Paul as he struggled with the heavy door. It didn't budge, and ramming his shoulder into the door was hurting him.

The snake maiden was closing the distance as it slithered over the bookcase and over the wood floor. A dreadful distorted moan, followed by a hiss, filled the hall, as it was only six feet away from Paul, who gave up on the door and dodged as the snake maiden plunged its sword arm into the door.

Paul, however, was safe for now, watching in horror as the beast wiggled its knife arm out from the wood door. Paul crawled farther back in the room, where dark figures huddled around, but he ignored them. The back of the snake maiden suddenly burst. A forty-millimeter round of some sort punched into its white flesh, showing black underneath. The round was louder on impact. Paul's ears were ringing from the pop, which turned out to be a propelled fragmentation grenade. The ungodly thing had absorbed most of the damage and shrapnel.

Paul had heard brief pops just before it happened and realized it was another gun. Automatic fire flooded the hall, and black chunks of flesh flew from the beast as it hissed and thrashed around. Its tail whipping around had crashed through the door, busting it outwards. The wood and metal shattered into pieces. The beast was wincing from every shot and soon retreated onto the wall and crawled back up into the ceiling, defying gravity. A man came rushing in with an assault rifle. It was Alonzo, who turned to help Paul up from the floor.

"Get out! Hurry! They're coming back." Alonzo urged Paul out the smashed door leading to an outdoor balcony. Alonzo withdrew a plastic square object from his bag.

"What are you doing?" asked Paul, as he trembled at the sight of two snake maidens emerging once again from the dark library.

"I got it from Maverick. Only one we had. Get down!" Alonzo planted a claymore mine down on the floor. The directional blast aimed toward the snakes. Alonzo had just enough time to arm it but not enough time to get more distance from it before the snakes were on him. The mine had done its job and detonated right on the snakes. The yellow flash filled the gloomy gray dust cloud that sprang up from the concussive force. Alonzo was on the safe end of the bomb, but the pressure spat him out the door, and he plowed into Paul. Paul's head hit the portcullis on the outdoor walk, with Alonzo on top of him. The bomb blast scattered projectiles and easily cut through the wood supports in the open part of the library. The ceiling caved in, bringing only some of the stone wall down. The explosion blew out a hole in the floor. Paul and Alonzo were unconscious, but the threat was gone, only for a while.

10

Amanda caught the gaze of a person standing in front of her, blocking the background light of the body. The person was talking in a cool, elegant manner that posed no threat. Was it the distant murmurings of her mother? A friend? She couldn't tell—and then she was suddenly awakened by a hand fiercely shaking her, and soon after, another hand cupped her mouth. The man standing over her was Don. His face was rigid and serious but also slightly shaken. His other hand pressed a pointed finger to his lips to indicate total silence.

It was something so urgent that Don didn't want to risk waiting until Amanda woke up. He feared she would make a noise. Don did not release his grip until after he carefully slid Amanda down from the bed to the floor. She nodded to signal she would remain calm and not scream. The room was a little better lit, as it was already dawn. Don must have fallen asleep as well because he hadn't awakened Amanda to take over his shift—this much already told her something had gotten in a while ago. The air reeked, and she was cold to the bone, as if she'd been thrown in a garbage pit during an early morning dew frost. The side of the barracks room that was the most illuminated revealed a shocking discovery. The scratches in the wood floor ran five feet from the door that was once blocked shut with the wrought-iron brazier. The heavy, impossible-to-move piece was now thrown back nearly where it had been, and the door was wide open, letting in the cold of outside.

"How did that not wake us up?" whispered Amanda.

Amanda came to realize that a force might have pulled it away slowly from the inside, without any sudden bump or rattle. Don pointed to the other door with the hatchet lodged underneath. They slowly begin creeping to the closed door, keeping a keen eye on the iron weapon racks and beds Don had thrown into the stairwell before resting. Nothing seemed to have left or entered through there either, but Amanda was not going to stick around to see what moved the iron brazier. Don did his best to open the door quietly, making only a few creaks that seemed very loud. The exit seemed safe, with nothing on the wall outside and more sunlight peering over the forest treetops. Don hunched down to secure the ax and gestured for Amanda to hurry along. Outside, they could see nothing below in the mist of the courtyard and garden or anything on the other walls.

"Okay, so let's—" Don's plan was severed by a black menacing doglike figure crawling up the side of the parapet wall, up and over the battlement, and flying straight into him, just as he turned back from looking at Amanda. The four-legged creature was the same as those from the horde that had swarmed the lower levels of the castle in the vault room. Amanda screamed as it tackled him backward. Its feet, on powerful hind legs, clawed at the stone from underneath. Don struggled to keep its pointed claws from tearing into him. The hands were small, and the claws were so long that Don had to secure them first.

Amanda acted finally after the shock of it and shoved the dagger blade in the demon's head. She extracted it and came down with it again, piercing the demon in the back. Only irritated, the beast turned to slap her away. She stumbled backward over the ledge. She shifted her weight quickly to keep from flying over the edge of the forty-foot wall and caught herself by grasping a bulky stone, just as her feet slipped from the eroded lip. The courtyard below seemed forever down, especially with the light mist covering the ground.

Don took advantage of the distraction and was able to free a hand for the ax, which he planted in the demon's slick face. It gave a nasty growl and violently lashed outward, away from him. He got up in time to run back to the door. Don had hoped to secure a larger weapon he'd seen just inside the barracks. Just as he got to the door, he froze, as the black-dressed figure of a woman with a tar-tainted face sprang up from the crevasses in the floorboards. She blocked the doorway with her terrorizing gaze, soaking wet dress, and blackness running from her flesh. In her hand was a larger ax with a broad blade used for executions back in that medieval time period.

The sudden fright from the woman sprouting from the floor was enough to make Don fall backward, away from the sight of it. The monster behind him was flailing around, fighting to free the hatchet from its face. The raggedy, sullen woman was slowly advancing on Don as he crawled away. The other door from the next tower was banging noisily, which meant more company. The metal bolts were punched out from each intense ramming from whatever was trying to break through. Amanda kept yelling at Don to get up with a strained voice.

The red-eyed maiden in a tar-burdened dress came up with her ax over Don and let out a slight chuckle. Don rolled to the left just as the black ax head struck the stone wall. He had rolled over the ledge and now was parallel with Amanda, who looked over at him helplessly. The door above broke open, releasing more of those demons that hopped along the wall as if frogs were let loose from a jar. Don could only afford Amanda one word, as his strength was quickly failing him.

"Jump." He shifted his eyes downward. She took notice and glanced down, seeing the body of water below her. *That's right!* she thought. The pond was just below and deep enough in the garden. She had to muster the courage to let go, but when the next demaon looked over the lip with its one eye and snapping jaws, she released and fell freely down. Her last glimpse of Don was turned to murky darkness. The water, frigid as ever, came up and around her, encompassing her. The shock was like being zapped by electronic currents. She crashed through at an odd angle, which hurt but perhaps was for the best, as there was only a few more feet of depth below her. She swam to the top to fill her lungs with the stagnant air. The garden around her seemed to have died. The flowers were shriveled, and leaves had fallen.

The garden was always maintained, but now there were no signs of life in any plant. Her attention quickly fell back to Don, who let go of the ledge and leaped off in such a way that he would surely hit the water. One of the monsters had grabbed him by the mouth slipped off and fell soon after. The other demon caught itself and crawled along the inside of the wall rapidly, in a dizzying way. The one that had fallen shifted into the bushes but soon shot off in another direction. Amanda, on the guard with her dagger in the one hand, kept a close watch on the dead, burned thistles.

Now, as the wind settled and the monsters up top stopped screaming, she snapped back to the pond. Don should have made it up by now.

"Millar! Millar!" Amanda was more scared than ever. "Don!" She screamed it over again, with ripples of fear washing over. She ran into the water, combing the surface with her arms. "*Don!*"

There were bubbles and light splashes but no human breaking through the surface of the water, fighting for air. Don did not come up, but what did was a different being—a human to be sure, but this human did not look to have been in the water. It was a burned body of a man with black, crackled skin, and no clothes on. He seemed to be crawling out from the water and stood up almost immediately. Not looking like he was going to keel over dead, he instead yelled in a terrifying shriek and ran from the pond. Another burned body and then another soon emerged from the pond. Amanda was in total awe and soon backed off all the way to the black fence that kept her from going any farther. People were screaming from the water as they charged through in hordes, all from a little pond—no clothes, no hair, or any recognizable features, just bodies without noses, eyes, lips, or even genitals.

They didn't seem to mind Amanda or didn't bother to communicate as Amanda tried to tell one to stop. Her voice was drowned out from the damnation of what they were suffering. The beings ran past her, frantically trying to get away from something she could not see. Another body of a woman came running out, crying. Her skin was like a gray volcanic ash with canyons of magma-red cracks in her brittle flesh. Some of her hair was showing on her head but only a little. Amanda could see that these things were just as scared as she was, if not even more on a level she could never comprehend. They were blind as well, with no cognition or sense of where they were going. They ran into the fence but quickly learned the way out, closer to the inner castle walls.

To her surprise, one of the retreating women was suddenly cut in two from the waist. Amanda instantly crouched low into the weeds, observing the large curved weapon that split the frantic woman—a scythe as long as five feet, with notches in the worn black steel. Then she noticed the black legs of a spider. The legs were tall; all eight zigzagged up fifteen feet to a body that was nothing but a pile of decaying heads and skulls. Amanda had thought they were eggs but they were heads of men and skulls alike, stuck together to make the body of the spider. The sockets of each leg were the mouths on the dead heads, making it look as if the legs were coming out of the throat. Amanda had never seen anything so morbid.

This thing was massive, and Amanda's eyes continued to journey up the snakelike spine of the creature that now had the body of a human skeleton, only with a larger rib cage. Its arms swayed out, clutching the harvester blade in complete silence. Its head was hidden, as it was covered with a cowl or ratty hood. Its gaze was not seen, as the head whipped around for more souls. Amanda could see only dark within the hood that was draped over its wormy black bones. The curved blade quickly made work of the fleeing humans burned to a crisp. None of them were in the right sense to figure out how to open the door into the main castle; rather, they ploughed into the wall. The half-spider/half-giant skeleton shuffled toward them in the training yard. A large, sweeping cut cleaved three of them like butter.

Amanda watched in horror as one tried to double back, but the one spider leg lifted and came down, impaling her from the head down through the groin and back into the mud. The leftover cadavers of the people instantly turned to ash and were lifted into the air, waving like a silky gray ribbon. The ashes were sucked into the black void of the hood. The creature was done harvesting the getaway souls and now made its way up the side of the castle to the roof and disappeared behind the tower. By this time Amanda was well on her way in the other direction along the inner castle wall. She ran along the stone toward the north end of the castle, leaping over wild branches and black vines that grown out over the course of the night.

When she reached the corner she broke down crying, as the thought of Don not making it out of the pond was crushing to her. The only person who could have helped was gone. She put her back against the wall and looked up at the bleak gray sky. The note she had picked up in the duke's study room crossed her mind. She produced the thinly worn paper from her pocket and studied it again.

The diagram sketch was a structure base and a tower erected up from that. There was an eight-pointed star at the tip of the tower. Amanda could tell it was some sort of map, and her best guess was that this object was located in the Weeping Tower.

Amanda's thoughts were soon edged out by a ghastly scraping noise—metal against stone—and it was getting closer. The squawk of a crow startled her as she was readying her dagger. She couldn't see what it was but had to force herself to peek. Her breath was steam in the menacing cold of the day. She inched out slowly, only allowing herself to look with one eye at the sound. It was a large ax blade dragging against the stone wall, with two feet and one arm holding the ax handle.

It was too bizarre to see only half of a being walking, but to Amanda's terror, the black wrought-iron fence that ran parallel with the wall was dissipating and manifesting into a humanlike creature that wielded the ax. The black mist quickly formed into the witch that attacked Don on the wall. Her eerie grin revealed little sharpened teeth, a face covered with dozens of scratches, and black tar hair tangling down her shoulders. Her eyes were red and locked on Amanda. The witch kept walking slowly, giving Amanda enough time to think of where she was going next. The north end door leading into the hall was just ahead. The door was usually locked but Amanda had kept the key on her from work. She was lucky Paul's crew had let her keep her keys. She opened the door gently, as she wanted to check the interior of the hall. It was dark, but some outer light crept in, revealing the two doors on the right. Strangely, the door to the old baths was open.

Just as Amanda walked in, she had to quickly step back out. Her heart raced when she caught a glimpse of a black being floating above the floor. Its face was white with a beak-like nose and gaping, droopy eye sockets. The black hooded robe it wore was ratty and in shredded tatters where it dangled just above the bloody floor. Now back outside, Amanda could see the witch come around the corner, with just fifty feet to go.

"Shit," she whispered to herself. Amanda had to look inside again; she had to lose the croaking lady dragging the ax. Inside, the hovering ghost creature was facing away from her and floating down the opposite way. However, this was bad. Amanda made an immediate right to take the long way up the stairs to the second level. She did not know what the ghost was capable of doing, so she kept away. Part of the way up the steps she fell to her knees, as a shrieking laugh froze her muscles. She didn't know if she was caught, but the laugh sounded nearly human and echoed from the baths. The silent ghost surprisingly did not turn around but floated the rest of the way down, ignoring the person staggering out of the bathroom. Amanda could not believe it. It seemed like everything that was happening was just another surprise, and nothing made any sense.

It was the body of a man, large in muscle mass and covered in blood. The man's head was hanging backward, exposing a red mushy neck that had been cleanly cut by something. Amanda was slowly clambering up the stairs, trying to turn away. The head was laughing hysterically, with the body flailing around. She recognized it as Fang, the Russian from whom she had escaped hours ago. His mouth moved within a head similar to a PEZ dispenser; it made no scientific sense at all. The unearthly laugh ceased when the black-tar witch lunged from the outer doorway, with the ax head digging into his chest. The force knocked the body back to the floor. The witch was hard at work, hacking up the remnants of Fang, with each swing clipping off a limb and chunks from the torso. Amanda was now totally out of sight and moving much more quickly into the knight's quarters. The floor was prepped for the exhibit, with the doors to each room open, revealing the standard and ornate living conditions of the thirteenth century warrior. The silence was bad enough. Not even peace in this place was comforting.

Amanda saw no signs of danger as she cautiously walked down the corridor, but she was somewhat disturbed by the mannequin statuettes dressed in knightly garb and suits of armor. They didn't move, but Amanda kept a steady watch on each. The curse played tricks on the mind, and Amanda knew that. It frightened her to think that if she were to die here, she might end up like Fang and come back as a half-mutilated lunatic.

She glanced back to ensure the witch was not following her. The large arched opening ahead led into the next barren chamber that smelled of burned wood. The stairwell was blackened from a recent fire, and to her left was the library, totally obliterated. She knew it had to have been the two center supports that failed and caused the ceiling to collapse. Shelves were knocked over and a tangled pile of broken beams and scattered brick blocked her way. To see this would normally have ruined her, but this place could be leveled now, and she would not care.

It was gone, lost in this evil curse that had destroyed it when the secret was out.

Amanda had to get through somehow. She stepped over splinters of wood and shell casings from a rifle.

Paul's gang was here in a fight. One that he most likely lost, she thought. She could see that the rest of the library was unscathed, and she could make her way around the ruins. She heard shuffling and quickly turned to it but saw that it was only a book with its pages flipping in the light draft coming in from somewhere. She still had to fight to traverse the library, stepping over giant bookshelves and beams. If this much of the library was gone, that meant the foundation for the tower would be partially unstable. Amanda knew she had to be quick about it. Whatever it was that Lamonthe had hidden up there was key to escaping. Escape, however, would be difficult, with the lingering danger of Paul's group in the way. Amanda stopped just before leaving the library to the sound of voices just outside on the balcony. The light poured in from the exit at the east end of the hall. She recognized the sound of two men speaking—it was Paul and Alonzo.

How did they not see what was happening on the east wall just now? Amanda figured they had just woken up and decided to hold while they figured out their next move.

Paul's head was pounding, but he was alive and well. His strength was dulled, but he was still intent on getting to the top of the tower. Alonzo helped him up.

"Glad to see you're awake. You wouldn't believe what I saw just now."

"Christ, it's morning already!" Paul was worried. "The chopper! Did it show?"

Alonzo shook his head. "Did you not hear it over the comms or by air? The blast knocked me out for I-don't-know-how-long, but I was here pulling guard while you recovered."

Paul was angry. "You should have gone the rest of the way! To signal the pilot!"

Alonzo stood his ground and glared at Paul.   "I don't have the map, *cabrón*. I have no clue where I am, and I just saved your sorry ass, so the least you can do is thank me."

Paul gritted his teeth and turned to check the radio. "Mav, come in. Rubio, come in!" Paul looked over at Alonzo. "Did you see them when you left the chapel?"

"They were there. I just did a comms check an hour ago but got nothing."

Paul rubbed the top of his head, wincing at the pain. "Damn that blast. What the hell was that?"

"A mine from Maverick's bag," said Alonzo.

"Gotta love that crazy bastard," said Paul. "Those rounds from your rifle ... how?"

Alonzo ejected a magazine to inspect the remaining cartridges. "Holy water. I blessed the rounds with holy water," he said.

Paul was speechless, but it didn't surprise him. It all made sense. These beings were truly from hell, and no amount of firepower would stop them permanently. This was going to be a battle between light and dark. Paul wasn't so sure if he had a light side.

"Hey, amigo, sorry about Jill." Alonzo had seen her

mangled on the floor when he aided him. Paul frowned at the thought of it. He then made a second attempt at getting them on the radio. And then a faint noise was heard not from the speakers but from the direction of the cathedral. It was instrumental, a musical hum. What an odd sound amid the wailing cries of fear and slaughter. The sounds were flat, repetitive high and low notes. The dark music playing was similar to a piano but much louder. Paul looked horrified as he glared wildly at Alonzo for some answer. He finally blurted, "The chapel!"

They took off down the outer balcony leading to the southeast wall, where the cathedral emitted a noise that had to be investigated.

11

The gloomy inside of the cathedral was still partially lit with the sconces and candles, now dripping wax vigorously all over the burgundy carpet atop the stone floor. The gloom from outside was not enough to saturate the dark stained-glass windows. Mav was startled by a sudden noise. He hadn't seen Rubio move from his laptop in a long while, but there was someone in the organ room, playing the age-old instrument. The deep tones sounded dreary, like a funeral dirge, but not sloppy or crude in anyway. Rubio took notice as well and stood up. Mav racked one round in his shotgun and gave Rubio the hand signal to stay there. He reached over with one hand to call out on his radio.

"Paul, come in. We got someone in the chapel with us. What's the report on that chopper?" The music went on, with a repetitive chorus. Rubio readied his MP5 submachine gun as Mav came upon the door that was slightly open. Inside the dim room were two candle stands on either side of a young blonde girl in a white gown. Mav couldn't believe it.

"Cohen!" Thinking it was Amanda, he firmly shouldered his shotgun but was stopped by Rubio right behind him.

"Cohen has black hair; that's not her," said Rubio.

Mav, already irritated, told Rubio to watch his back and then called out to the girl. "Hey you, who are you?" His voice was almost drowned out by the loud organ music. The girl's face was hidden, but nothing seemed abhorrent about her. She had curves and smooth white skin. Her gown was clean and untouched by the taint around her. Mav found himself getting closer, with his shotgun stooping low but still within his grasp. The tune of the music changed into something brighter but kept the same dreaded sound with every other note.

"Paul, can you hear me? Damn, these radios are shit. You there, what are you doing here?" Mav dared himself to get closer but realized she was not making any move to take note of him. Mav decided to grab her on the shoulder to get her attention, but just as he did it, she changed in a blink. Her dress remained white but was soiled as if it had weathered over time. Her hair was knotted and had thinned, and her skin became pale, with blotches of black and random cuts on her arms. The music stopped, and Mav was already regretting that he had disrupted her. Her head spun around on her shoulders and let out a demonic howl, mixed with a womanly scream. Her face was white with black, beady eyes and black veins within the surface of her deathly flesh. Her teeth were sharpened down to little points, like the witch who'd gone after Amanda and Don.

Mav, only a couple of feet away, was locked with panic as the thing spun around with one sweeping motion of her arm, which held a broad sword. It was not one that had been on display but one used for actual felling. The blade was sharp enough to put a sizable gash in Mav's belly. Mav made a slight attempt to dodge, but the tip of the sword still got him as he fell backward. He began shuffling back in a panic, kicking his legs out to propel himself. He felt his breathing grow heavy as his anxiety took over. The twisted lady stood up, with her head rotating back to the right position and her legs shuffling under her gown. She was barefoot as well, and she turned the carpet black where she stepped, as if death were within her. Her crazed scream turned into a sadistic laugh as she walked closer to Mav, who was now outside the room. The top part of her gown around her neck was splattered with bright red blood and trickled down her lips, as if she had just eaten flesh.

The image was truly shocking to Mav. She carelessly flailed her sword from side to side with her two unskilled hands, laughing all the while, like a child having fun with it. Mav managed to get one shot in her belly, pushing her back some. Rubio took action and charged at her, pushing her back into the room when the sword was off to one side. He slammed the door shut and held it, using his weight. Inside, they could hear the more laughter as the door began jolting under Rubio. It jumped and cracked, but he was determined to keep the creature inside, even if it exhausted him. Mav was in shock as he examined his bloody wound.

"Get the hell out of here!" shouted Rubio.

"I need … help … I can't fucking walk!" said Mav, grabbing the podium as some sort of support. His bloody hand struggled to get a grip, but it made the wood slippery. The door Rubio was holding began to turn black, as if the wood was being burned, but no signs of fire were present. The black made a silhouette outline of the woman, who did not reappear from the door itself. Slowly, her face and arms morphed through the wood as Rubio inched backward, nearly paralyzed with fear. The woman spawned through the door and resumed her onslaught. Mav steadied his shotgun and fired. The blast this time took out a chunk of her head and her right eye. Mav was shocked as she kept laughing, with little black widow spiders crawling out from the hole in her head and running over her face.

With one hand she stretched her arm out at an astonishing length of six feet. Her hand latched onto Rubio's face, who was not expecting the action. Rubio grabbed at her arm, trying to pry it away as her monstrous claws pressed into Rubio's cheeks. He sacrificed one hand to reach for his MP5, once again slung on his shoulder. If he waited any longer, the pressure of her hand closing would crush his skull. Rubio pressed the muzzle to her wrist and shot a burst, severing the hand from the rest of the elongated arm. The witch seemed unmoved by the act and laughed even harder. Her chilling voice ranted something obscene as the air cooled to freezer temperature. While Rubio slowly ripped the hand away, she used the other hand and flung the broad sword straight into Mav's chest without any effort. Mav gagged on some blood and keeled over, with eyes like saucers staring into oblivion. The sword's end shown through the backside, covered in red.

Rubio finally came to his senses after throwing the twitching hand off to the side. Five bloody gashes were left etched on the sides of his face, but he managed to aim his weapon. The thing noticed within a second and sporadically made a deafening croak. The hellish being erupted into a web of black slimy strands and extended all over the cathedral in every direction. Her body was morphed into hundreds of these strands, like Silly String. It instantly latched onto Rubio and restrained him from moving, like a fly caught in a web. His neck, feet, and arms were wrapped in the slime that was hot, like burning wax. Rubio still had one hand on his gun, now pointed to the ceiling. The woman's head was all that was left; it was suspended in air with her hair acting as the black stringy slime attached to the cluster of web. It twisted toward Rubio and spoke in a patronizing and ghastly tone.

The voice was like a sweet lady but distorted and toxic. "Do you like fire? Your sister likes fire."

Rubio knew it was over, but this thing was going back where it came from. The strands around his neck were choking him, but he still had the strength to twist his gun hand in a way that it aimed toward the lit chandelier. He grimaced. "Do you like fire? Bitch." He squeezed the trigger. A burst of automated rounds peppered the anchor in the high ceiling. The weight of the iron chandelier pulled it down, with its candles falling all over the webs. The object tore through most of the strings, and the fire followed the strands throughout the web as if it were oil. The flames licked up the black stringy maze and spread quickly. Rubio caught fire and screamed from the burning pain. The room was so bright that when Paul barged in, he had to shield his eyes from the light and heat.

The noisy screech of the demon was loud but Rubio's

cry was piercing. Paul realized it was over for him and ended his misery with a single gunshot to Rubio's head. Alonzo grabbed Paul and pulled him away, back into the foyer of the cathedral. Paul was seething with rage.

"What happened? I thought they couldn't get in there!"

Alonzo tried examining the inside that was quickly falling apart. "Boss, I ... I don't see Mav either." They stood back from the doorway as more smoke drifted out. Wood cracked and bended to the rage of the fire spreading over all the benches and carpets.

Paul cursed and screamed as he threw his radio into the brick. Furiously he charged for Alonzo, who had his hands up in surrender. "How did they get in the church? Idiot! Where is your God, huh?" He threw Alonzo back into the wall but then let go of him. Paul fell to his knees in despair. His hands spread flat in the black muck that was spilled by something or seeped through the rock.

Alonzo looked at him helplessly, as if there was nothing left of Paul. Just a beaten-down bum, ranting the same thing over and over. As the crackling of the fire dwindled, the sound of a *whopping* noise beat the air. To their relief, it was the sound of a distant helicopter. The whirring hum of the engines grew louder overhead.

"He just showed up," said Alonzo. Paul lifted his head, and Alonzo helped him to his feet. "Check your ammo." Paul examined his magazine, and Alonzo said, "I have a half a mag left. What about you?"

Paul shook his head. "Enough to get to that tower. Whatever is in our way, we smash through it. You got it?

No slowing down for anything. I'm getting the fuck out of here."

Alonzo looked around as the black tar on the floors began to move. The crevices in the stone walls grew black vines. They had wound together to make fingers and then arms, and then the strands started weaving together to make twisted bodies of those demon dogs they had fought in the catacombs. Dozens of hellions were spawning quickly to populate the castle and devour anything earthly.

"We better move fast." Alonzo's advice was well spoken, and the two quickly sprinted across the courtyard and into the main hall of the gloomy structure.

Step by step, Amanda carefully advanced along the stony steps that zigzagged up a stairwell landing on the third tower floor of the castle. The room was illuminated by sunlight flooding in through two archery slits on either side. This part of the tower was currently used as storage—old exhibit furniture and other crates stashed along with maintenance equipment. The stairs ahead of her were simple wooden beam stairs, spiraling along the inside walls another thirty feet up, where it led to the upper chamber of the tower.

Amanda hated this part of the castle, as it always had seemed unstable. When they had first uncovered it, the stairs leading up were fractured stone that was eroding and chipped badly. Almost twelve tons of it were removed by hand to reduce pressure on the lower levels. The LPS installed wooden steps instead. The tower was found to be sitting at a ninety-five degree angle, which was bad enough and led to hours of debate among the project leads as to how they would remedy it.

Amanda knew Paul would head back to the tower, so she had to make it quick. *A helicopter? Asshole thinks he can get away?* Whatever it was back at the cathedral, she hoped it ended them there. Just as she was about to step forward on the first stair, hands reached out and grabbed her arm. Quickly she twisted, but before her scream could be heard, another hand cupped her mouth tightly. A man emerged from the shadows, holding her firmly against the beam of the stair supports.

"Amanda, it's me. Quiet ... please."

Her heart raced, and her eyes widened. It was Don, with dried mud streaked across his face and a pungent odor to match the look. She exploded inside with joy and relief as she hugged him. He pulled away quickly to link eyes with her.

"Shhh, keep it down."

"I thought you were gone."

"I know, I know."

Amanda was nearly in tears. "I thought I was going to be alone. I was scared." Her smile left and she couldn't help but cry, and Don embraced her again to calm her down.

"Look," he said, clutching her shoulder, "we need to get up top. You hear that?" The faint sound of the helicopter was cutting in high and then low, as if it was circling the area. She nodded. "The pilot is trying to find a place to land. We have to—"

"No. No, Don, it's Paul's ride out of here. They'll shoot us. I have another plan."

This boggled Don's mind. *How could she know that?*

She took the first two steps leading up, but Don grabbed her again. She froze and her eyes intensified with irritation as she looked at him. Don lifted a finger, signaling to wait as he grabbed a broomstick from the corner; it had a broken shard of mirror taped to the end. He had her follow up three-quarters of the way, and then he began to crawl slowly a few more steps. Don extended the handle with the mirror as far as he could go. The mirror bounced around as Don steadied the handle and crept from the floor above the next landing. The mirror revealed a few things on the next floor, which was the duke's master room. In the sunlight coming in through the balcony doors was a lanky figure that Amanda recognized as the spider with the giant skeleton upper body, the soul harvester that sucked the spirits of the that were fleeing. The hooded cowl faced away from the mirror. The human heads acting as the body were moving their mouths. It was so grotesque that Amanda felt sick, especially because of the eight that had the legs emerging from the mouths as if they were sockets. What poor choices had they made to be a part of that monster? It had not moved at all.

"It is attracted to sound," whispered Don. He held up a bloody hand radio. "I found this on some messed-up guy in the hall. One of Paul's guys. The battery is still charged, but only one channel comes in clear." Don then gave the hand radio to Amanda. She knew he must have gotten it off Fang. "When I tell you, turn the radio on, and set it in the window seal down there, but not yet; only when I tell you."

"What are you going to do?"

"I'm going to watch where this thing goes. If it turns toward us, we have to leave, but I saw it crawl in through the outside doors, so it might leave that way."

Amanda nodded, understanding what she had to do. She crept back down the stairs and placed the radio on the seal of the open window. The cool, clammy mist made her hand colder with all the sweat from her palms. She noticed the volume was at max. The channel was set to one. Don finally held up two fingers. Amanda's heart raced as she turned the knob to two. The most repulsive moaning and screaming came from the speaker. It shattered the total silence and drove her mad. The hellish sounds were picked up on a certain frequency—the things that were yet to come, Amanda was sure of it. Don observed the spider creature shuffle around once. Its giant sickle blade was in one bony hand. The black void of the cowl scanned the room and then suddenly the legs shifted up the side of the wall and stood upside down on the ceiling. The frightful taps of each spider leg striking the surface moved to the outer walls.

The distraction worked, and the beast was out through the balcony. Don waved Amanda over frantically. She scurried up the stairs, quickly but silently.

"The highest room in the castle. This is where it is," said Amanda.

Don looked confused. "Where *what* is?"

"The key." She laughed under her breath. "Jesus, Donny, what the hell happened to you?"

Don took a seat on the chest at the end of the bed. He took a deep breath and started fidgeting with his hands nervously. "Well, I can't quiet explain. On the wall ... after I fell in the pond and was in the water, I saw you get out, but I felt hands grab my legs and ankles. The pond is not that deep, but it felt like the hands were dragging me down forever. Other people were swimming past me, racing to the surface. Naked and burned. God, I thought ... is this some sort of nightmare? I looked down through the depths to see if there was a bottom, but instead it was like a vast, dark ocean below me. I saw a glow, like a volcano with magma or something, but it was like fire under the water. I saw it; I saw hell and the souls trying to swim away from it. I thought about my family. I thought how my job was not over and that I had to get out. So I cried out to God. With nothing else to save me, it was all I could think of.

"I never once considered any of it to be real but another hand reached down. It had this ... light around it, an aura. The hand reached in, and I reached for it. The feel of it pulling me up was like I was being flung through time and space, but finally my head broke the surface. I coughed up so much water and lay there until I had the strength to get up. I tracked your footprints back inside. How am I going to explain any of this without sounding crazy? If I make it out of here alive with you, my next fear is trying to come to terms with all this. I will never look at everything so logically again because what I have seen ... is not logic; its madness."

Amanda knelt down next to him. She handed him a piece of worn yellow paper. "Even madness has a way.

That's what I kept from Paul and his crew. It's what I found in the old study in the cellar."

Don was amazed; his lips formed a grin. "This is a map of the lower level. It looks a lot bigger on this though. What gives?"

"Many of the catacombs were either sealed off or caved in; that's why it seemed short from here to here," she said, using her finger as a guide. She then pointed to the area at the end of the vault. "This little chamber we did not see because there is a door there that was hidden. Lamonthe made a reference note on a spell that was cast on the seal of the door. He was going to escape through that hidden passage because he knew his men would try to kill him. He was planning for that after his wife rose from the dead, but it didn't go as planned."

"So what now? Is it a physical item we are looking for? A key, you said?"

"No, a spell of some sort. Lamonthe wrote that he kept it close to his wife. His wife was bedridden right here."

"What if it was kept on her and not in this room?"

Amanda was frantically searching, having doubts. She feared Don would lose patience. The sound of the helicopter grew.

That reminded Don of something else. "The chopper— you said it was Paul's?"

"I overheard them talking. An outside source they had reached earlier. Chances are, they are going to pick them up here. Ditch the equipment for sure. They're running scared."

"They'll still kill us when they get the chance. We better move."

Amanda took a breath and tried to think. Everything in the room was wiped clean and examined. Her notes only mentioned where the bed was placed from the indentions in the wood that fit the correct measurements of the frame. There was even some discoloration in the wood from where the legs had sat for years. Why was she thinking about the bed? She referred back to the note Lamonthe left.

"Just go back over the clues if you have to. I hear that thing moving again," said Don.

The writing was faded and nearly impossible to completely decode.

"The only thing that I caught was, '*the key which was left by my queen's side, above all that I do preside. From blood and stone I hide, the power to move earth …*' It's all a blur from there, and then down here …" She indicated the last words. "'*With peace at last, from the ground, our love is yet to bloom once more.*' But this man has no love. He committed atrocities in his own land." Amanda crouched by the bed and table. The glass display case showcased an amulet made of silver. The necklace was in the shape of a heart, with an inlay of a golden sun. The very same sun that was the main symbol for Lamonthe's banner. It was the family badge. The black sun was his castle. The gold sun was his wife. "He had a love for his wife only, everything else was chaos to him," she said. "The gold was that of Satan's demands. Apart from the ritual. He needed it untouched, undisturbed …"

Don almost laughed. "Look where that ended up."

"He hated this place and wanted to leave but not without her. This necklace was the only thing we found up here worth any value, but it was forgotten."

Don was getting anxious. The chopper grew louder. "Cohen ..."

She ignored him. "The spell is that of love! In a panic, Lamonthe fled to the vault with his wife's body. He forgot this piece of her that he made with this last piece of gold. The gold sun is what he needed, and before Paul or anyone came, we were the first to come across it. I can't believe we didn't see it!"

Despite their situation Amanda figured it out, and in her excitement she took the butt of her dagger and struck at the glass to the display case.

"Amanda, wait!" The shattering sound was louder than usual and attracted some unwanted attention. Realizing what she had just done, she froze with terror as Don rushed toward her.

The tapping of the spider legs surrounded them. Don leaped and tackled Amanda to the bed. The scythe blade came piercing through the fine crease of the stone like it was nothing. A five-foot blade of black, scorching steel extracted and pierced through another area of the wall. Amanda quickly got back up and grabbed the silver-and-gold heart necklace while Don pulled her away from the balcony entrance; a spider leg swept in, just missing her. Another leg appeared and another, until the whole being angled through. Its massive figure stretched back out, with the twenty-foot ceiling just above its head. They didn't want to stay to see what it would do, but as they fled down the stairs, a shower of green fluid with a stench like vomit violated their senses.

The monster spat it out all over the room, and it acted as a corrosive acid that ate through stone and parts of the floor. It bled through and buckled the planks with the weight of the furnishings sitting on top. Some of it poured down onto the top steps, but ate through only part of it as it lost its potency. Don was not worried; they both flew down past the storeroom and finally to the ground floor level, near where the sublevel stairs were. Amanda stumbled and tripped from skipping too many steps, but Don caught her and helped her along.

12

The cellar entrance was right before them. Amanda's feet were swollen from the blistering and scarring the day before. The hellfire of the chain wrapping around her ankles seemed to have left a burning tinge that might never go away. That same grip of death was an experience revisited. Unfortunately for Amanda, it happened again, only this time it was no chain but a scaly dry tentacle wrapping around her waist. They were just about to head down the stairs when she was suddenly ripped away into the air. Her body hit the wall with a thud. Her feet were hanging above the floor.

"Amanda!"

"Don, help!" Her nerves were shot, and her muscles tensed to a point where she did not lose her grip on the dagger in her fist. The strange tentacle pulled her with immense strength around the corner of the center divider wall. The other side was the servant quarters and the kitchen beyond that. Not much light reached these rooms, as there were no windows. Amanda expected a machine that ground humans into pulp but was instead met with another demon-like creature that was terrifyingly different. It crouched on its hind legs, sitting sideways on the wall. Its head was more humanlike, but its mouth was abnormally open and stretched to allow for several long tentacles to whip out in every direction. Its eyes were evil red slits with ash-gray skin and four lanky arms that dug into the stone.

The noise it made was like static breathing, broken and similar to paper tearing, only with a shrill scream behind it all. Amanda was not sure what it was doing, but the creature was moving backward into the pitch-black kitchen. She had no intention of being the victim. She used her dagger to saw at the tentacle. The noise did not change, but the extremity shook violently as it became severed, and she fell free to the floor. However, there were more serpent-like tentacles flailing around. One smacked her over the face, knocking her to the side. Don raced around the corner as the creature leaped from the wall to the floor and closed in on Amanda. She was stunned for a moment; Don broke a chair over the hunched back of the slender beast.

It turned its bald head quickly toward the new aggressor while its extremities continued to probe and sniff at Amanda awkwardly. Don realized it was stronger than it appeared and felt that regret when it used one hind leg to buck him back seven feet. Don's back slammed into the farthest end of the room. He fell to his rear and tried to regain his strength from that blow.

The rooms were then filled with ear-pounding bangs and pops. In the dark, muzzle flashes flared. Two men advanced forward with weapons locked out. Alonzo's assault rifle rounds peeled gray flesh from the demon, showing off the black slimy tissue underneath. Paul's shots met with the tentacles and the creature's head. It jumped and jerked at each hit but hissed and finally withdrew. After all the shots it took, Don could not believe the speed at which it still moved. It jumped to the wall and leaped again through the opening to the back hall.

"I'm out!" shouted Alonzo, ejecting his magazine.

"I'm not," said Paul, checking his extended clip. "I got just enough for you bastards." He pointed it at Amanda.

Alonzo was past it all. "We need to just go! There are more trying to get in behind us. That blockade will not hold." The door back in the kitchen was banging and moving violently from a force on the other side.

"I'll start with you, Cohen," said Paul, ignoring Alonzo's shouts. His gun barrel was like a tunnel with no light at the end. At first Amanda squinted, anticipating the bullet. Then the noise came … the faint cackle Paul had just caught onto. He was delayed in his execution as he watched Amanda grit her teeth, unafraid at this point and reveling in her unseen victory.

She spit blood on his boots and managed to sit up. Her side was sore and her muscles frail, but for the first time in hours, she was excited. "You might want to save those shots."

Paul considered her words, but he had to ask. "For what?"

Don was still worried and held out his hand.

"You missed one," Amanda said.

Paul studied her glance that indicated the dark ceiling above. In the blackness were two glowing red eyes. A bit of light from the hall window intensified and revealed another demon body clinging to the rafters. A tentacle shot down and wrapped around his neck. Paul's face instantly turned red. Veins bulged from his forehead as the thing lifted him up, suspending him above the floor.

"C'mon, let's go now!" Don took the opportunity to retrieve Amanda. Alonzo ignored them and was contemplating leaving Paul, but he wanted to see if he would get out. The last three shots erupted but did nothing as the tentacle reeled him in toward the creature's jaws. The other tentacles retracted, giving room for several rows of snakelike fangs to protrude from the gums. Paul could feel the heat of its breath and saliva dripping on his head as he was inches away from being a snack.

Out of all Alonzo's cries, Paul managed to pay attention to one as he shouted from below.

"Use this—hurry! Catch!"

Paul was expecting a weapon of some sort but instead locked his fingers around an small wooden object with beads. Without overthinking it, Paul reached up with the rosary and pressed the cross into the beast's head. It sizzled on the flesh, like branding cattle. It let out a shrill howl and then a hiss as it released Paul. Like a frightened lizard, the demon vanished into the dark corners of the kitchen. He gagged and coughed. Alonzo helped him up hastily, pulling him at the same time.

"Catch a breath later, *cabrón*. We're leaving now!"

They fled up the stairs of the tower, leaving the rosary behind. The black accumulation of leaching fluid through the pores of the stone floor was forming even more ravenous things but much more quickly, and they shot out from the blackness that was pooling. They limped and trod up the stairs, with the wailing of ghastly things behind—cries of people mixed with what sounded like dogs growling and claws scratching away at the rough steps.

The two ran past the store room and panted their way up the long wooden stairs. Paul clearly was out of breath but somehow managed to find more when his fear set in. The floor below them exploded, with a pool of black and red demonic creatures swarming in like angry bees. "This is insane!" Paul's fear pushed him. He rushed ahead of Alonzo into the duke's chamber. The stairs creaked more with Alonzo's weight on the acid-eaten wood. On the second step from the top, he broke through.

"Ah shit!" His legs dangled below, but the Spaniard caught the top stair with his right hand.

"Hold on!" shouted Paul, turning back. Paul was stopped by the unusually spongy texture of the ground. His feet felt hot, and he noticed his boots were melting. A wet substance was soaking the floor, and it occurred to him why Alonzo had fallen through. Alonzo reached with his left hand to grab the wet lip of the floor. Paul tried to warn him but was too late, and the acid instantly melted his fingers. Alonzo shrieked with pain and cursed something in Spanish as he looked with horror at the flesh bubbling white, with bloody pus leaving nothing but a palm and a thumb. The rest of the stairs below him crumbled and fell from the acid and weight of monsters climbing up.

"*No*, don't leave! Help me!"

Paul was at a loss. He saw that whatever he was standing on would soon eat his feet to the bone, so he ran, leaving Alonzo for dead. The swarming horde began to pile on top of each other to gain height. They were determined to reach Alonzo and consume him. However, he looked down and decided there was another way. Being eaten alive by the damned was not an option. He let go with his good hand (also being slowly eaten away) to grasp the knife in his belt sheath. As he fell, he had enough time to withdraw it. His fall was broken by soft flesh and fur, things with gnashing teeth and torturous agendas. As Alonzo felt the biting, he plunged the combat knife into his own heart. The crew of tomb raiders was now down to the leader.

The next set of stairs leading up from the chamber was not as lengthy. Paul burst up through the trap door that let in sunlight and the chilling air of the day. He quickly threw the door shut and sat on it. He ripped his boots from his feet as he felt the nail-biting pain of burning. The chopper now was hovering low near the flat roof of the tower. It was a city-owned helicopter piloted by two men; another man stepped out of one door. The landing gear met with the surface, and *he* stepped off. The wind whipped his tie around relentlessly as he quickly approached Paul, who was yelling like a madman. The man who was taming his sports coat from flying around was none other than Phil Orrelle, the regional coordinator of LPS. He looked confused as Paul waved his arms frantically.

"We need to go now! Don't fucking land here, you idiot. Lift off now!"

Phil ignored his rant and was enraged. He shook his fist and barked at his subordinate. "You said you would have it ready by yesterday!" He shouted loud and clear over the roar of the chopper blades. "I thought I could count on you to get the prize, but instead you play me for a fool? Where is the rest of your team?"

Paul's eyes almost bulged from his head. "They're dead! They're all dead! Get in the … look out!" Paul reached past the corrupted employer to point at the pilots who were not expecting a swift end to their lives. From below, the curved sickle blade flew up and pierced the first pilot's head, splitting the helmet and cutting into the second pilot's neck and torso. The harvester was below, outside the tower wall. The curved blade was keeping the chopper from lifting. Phil's jaw dropped. The second pilot twitched and lost control of his arms, which were throwing the flight control sticks off course. The first pilot had a death grip on his control but shifted in the opposite direction when the sickle was pulled from his head. His limp body fell over, and the chopper's tail end lifted up first. Paul ran for it anyway but missed as the aircraft spun off instantly, spiraling viciously.

"*No-o-o!*" Paul's cry revealed his anguish better than words. Phil was paralyzed with fear. The chopper came back around full circle, slamming into the upper side of the tower, with its blade pelting the stone. Two remaining propeller blades flew off the rotary mount and over the roof. Phil did not anticipate the rapid decline as the chopper blade swept down, chopping him clean in half in the blink of an eye. One end of the debris snapped Paul's right foot nearly off his leg. He screamed, feeling the worst bit of excruciating pain wash through him. The chopper had blown to pieces and left a giant ball of black smoke billowing in its wake. It had also done a considerable amount of damage to the tower as it shifted and leaned farther over. The stone at the base cracked and made a severe fault in the structure. As the tower rocked, the trap door flew open. Paul rolled over on his back, wincing from his shattered leg.

The snarling demons came through the door and populated the roof, while Paul watched in horror. The smoke and char of the chopper lingered in the air. Paul had no ammo left and nothing to protect him. The tapping legs of the spider harvester crawled up over the ledge of the roof to claim its last soul. Paul tried inching his way back and pleaded with the monstrosity as it gazed through the blackness of the open hood. Silently, the beast moved closer and scooped up Paul with its long bony fingers. He wrestled and kicked the one good leg he had. Like a quick snack, the skeleton spider shoved Paul into the dark face of the hood. The yelling was like an echo within a cave as his feet stuck out. The beast crammed the rest of him in, and he fell into the dark oblivion. Though physically it was not possible, as there were only ribbed bones exposed on the outside, Paul's screams sounded as if he were in the depths of a great chasm.

The rest of the tower buckled from the weight and collapsed, with the center stonework bowing inward. Like a stack of dominoes, the upper part with all the monsters fell with the rock and sealed them within the dust plume.

Amanda felt the moving bodies under her feet as they progressed down into the wine cellar. In the entire castle, the basement level was the most transformed; it felt grungier than ever. Don had grabbed a lit torch from the wall. He couldn't believe he would find himself down there again, but he had to trust in Amanda. It was back to ground zero with the key—the amulet. Above, they paused as they heard the faint roar of the structure coming down. Dust from the ceiling sprinkled down. The stairwell went black as the rubble filled the cavity.

"We're closed off. I hope you have a plan," said Don.

Amanda didn't feel any more confident than he did. She kept going on blind faith. "This has to work. We need to move now."

The shifting walls became like a lucid dream. The torchlight only illuminated up to five feet around them. Don could hear the scampering sounds of the demons overhead and feel the wisps of some chilling ghostlike essence pass through them. The light made it hard to see past the bubble of luminance. Don tried his best not to look down at the floor. Infused with the stone and mud were the backs of people; an arm tried to reach for anything to clutch. Faces here and there were moving their mouths, but no sound was heard. Don suddenly felt his ears compress as most sound was eliminated. It started to feel like a space vacuum, only there was air to breath.

"What's happening? Why can't I hear?" asked Don, slowing down.

Amanda didn't have time to answer. She only tugged at his arm, urging him to press on. Amanda felt the brush of fur on her arm. She was praying for a safe passage to the vault, thinking that at any moment, one of the beasts would grab them. She figured the things were preoccupied with more of the escaped souls, as there were more screams all around them. People shouted in other languages and some in English, pleading for them to stop.

"Why aren't they attacking us?" shouted Don.

"They're busy, but we don't have much time."

They were halfway through the catacombs when things began to get chaotic. Amanda saw it so fast that it became a blur, but she would not forget the naked people halfway out of the mud, getting pulled back under, as their fingertips were the last thing showing. She was startled by the sight of tails whipping by and large bat wings fluttering in the fringes of the torchlight.

She nearly dropped the torch when a crazed man with ash-gray skin leaped in front of her. His eyes were hollow sockets, and his arms grabbed at Amanda's jacket. He was frantically yelling in what sounded like Latin. Amanda froze as Don tried to push him away. The expression on his cracked, dry face was one of desperation. This man was removed quickly, as two giant metal hooks looped inward into each eye socket. The hooks were at the ends of chains, similar to the grinder beast. The man screamed even louder when the hooks pulled his face and skull apart. His grip released Amanda, and demonic claws tore into the man's flesh, taking him apart like a jigsaw. Don had to reach for Amanda to pull her out of the way of more twisted demons claiming their prize.

It was not long before the halls were crowded with beings. The torchlight helped to distinguish them from the dead. Finally, Don and Amanda reached the end where the wall had been blown out. They squeezed through and stumbled into the vault, which was surprisingly empty.

Amanda was relieved, but Don was trying to find as much rubble as he could to block the opening.

"Come on; help me. They'll start to flood in soon," said Don, almost out of breath.

"They will get in anyway. The exit is just over here," said Amanda, pointing to the back. The vault was dark, but Amanda and Don made sure they walked around the gold pile. She studied the walls to look for some sort of unusual crease or discoloration, indicating a hidden door. Roots and vines had made their way through the stone over the years and now nearly tripped Amanda. There were so many vines and roots populating the back wall it was impossible to tell where the door was located. Her heart sank and anxiety kicked in.

"It's got to be behind here!" She started sawing at the vines with her dull-edged dagger. Don realized how futile it was as he waved the torch over the rest of the wall. Amanda now was upset as she violently slashed at the vines. Tears rolled down her eyes as she dropped, with the dagger hitting the cold ground. Don tried to burn the vines away, but the fire did not do anything as the vines were too damp with moisture. Don set the torch down and knelt beside Amanda to embrace her.

"We'll find a way. It's okay. We have to think."

She sniffled and rediscovered the heart amulet in her pocket. The glint from the torchlight highlighted the gold inlay. "What did I miss?" Amanda's question was left unanswered.

The dreary silence was confronted by the faint screams down in the catacombs. Don scrambled for his torch at the next sound, which shuffled where the gold was in the center of the room. To their amazement, the four pillars in the center lit up. The torches in the holders revealed the bloodied, melted gold and the skeletons of the four priests who were part of the damned ritual so long ago. Amanda did not know whether to be frightened or at peace. The figure from earlier, which had emerged from the gold when Paul triggered the curse, stood there once more. The liquid gold body of a man in the shape of a robe rippled with every movement. The face was even gold, as well as the eyes.

Only the contours outlined Hugues de Lamonthe's true appearance. The voice was a deep heavy sound that uttered something in French and then Latin. The sound was chilling yet calm. Finally, the ghostly figure shifted to English. "Are you the ones who came for my gold?"

Don was left speechless. It was not every day he was interrogated by a spirit.

Amanda, however, stepped forward and spoke with unfailing conviction. "We're not here for your gold! We were taken against our will. We mean no harm; we just want to leave. Tell those things to let us be!"

"The children of Satan have no boundaries and cannot be tamed. They are but part of an oath made with the master. Soon they will spread throughout the land and consume all that there is. The wolves will fight but will eventually lose." Amanda had figured the wolves sensed this threat in their area. It explained why they all formed around the castle. Animals always had a keen sense of survival.

"It doesn't have to be this way! Your lady, your wife, is in a better place. Look ... you forgot this." Amanda tossed the heart amulet into the gold pile. It made a slight change in the air as it hit, like a concussion from a blast miles away. The ground vibrated a few brief moments.

The dreaded voice shifted tempo, and now a sorrowful mourn took over. "She was all that I had." Amanda noticed another hand formed by gold rise up to secure the necklace in its fist.

"You wanted to escape. Just the two of you. Now let us go. Just the two of us!"

Lamonthe was silent for a moment. The blockade of rubble was being moved and punched out by the ravaging minions on the other side. Don knew they only had seconds.

"You have done this service to me. Now we are complete. Go, and never forget what belongs here."

It was an easy deal to which Amanda could agree. They noticed a shift in the walls behind them. The vines began to miraculously move and wiggle back into the crevasses of the cracked stone. Like an army of retreating snakes, the vines cleared a way to the stone door that was rolling over to the side. The scrapping of stone against stone was a beautiful sound in their ears. The sound of shrill roars and hissing behind them was not so welcome. Don dared to gaze over his shoulder at the sight of black things breaching the small opening, like ants. The demons were the first ones to scurry across the walls. The rolling door left two feet of opening for them to get through. Beyond that was a long hall with an incline.

It was a bit disheartening to not see any sunlight, but at least there was another way, rather than going back.

"Look for a switch! Anything to close this door!"

shouted Amanda. There was nothing. Just a bunch of roots and dirt. The tunnel was not structured in any sound way. The only thing that kept it from caving in were slab-cut stone supports halfway in the earthen walls. They were located a quarter of the way down and seen at certain intervals. The stone was cracked and looked brittle from no upkeep over the centuries.

"Right here!" said Amanda. "We can try to block the way!" She and Don started to pull at one crude bit of stone bulging out from the wall. It was pointless; they couldn't get it to even budge.

"Shit! It won't ... *aahhh*!" Don felt the sting of a sharpened object tear into his thigh. It was the most agonizing pain he had felt. The same hook on a chain had shot out from the blackness and snagged Don. The pull was violent, but Amanda caught him just in time with one arm. Don had a firm grasp on the stone pillar. His fingers were turning white from the pressure of gripping the stone.

Amanda noticed the pillar move a bit, but it was from the sheer force on Don, who was now suspended in the air.

"Hold on! Grab the stone!" Amanda told him to let her go and grab the pillar with both hands. The beast that had a hold on him was the dreaded grinder that had claimed Helena. The width of its maw took up the entire tunnel as its giant spike rollers spun around. A few rocks and boulders fell in and were smashed in the grinding steel mouth.

"It burns! Get it out!" shouted Don. Amanda knew the feeling but quickly felt more sympathy as the hook was buried in his hip. It pulled at the flesh, but did not rip it out. Amanda kept her wits about her and mustered all the strength she could to pull the hook from his leg. Her fingers that wrapped around the metal were burning. She realized she was not strong enough, but she had to tell Don the bad news. "You're going to have to let go."

He managed to open up his squinting eyes, realizing that Amanda might have gone crazy.

"Let go and grab the hook, but brace your feet in the dirt!" Amanda had to yell over the sound of the grinding. Before Don lost too much strength, he took the chance and let go of the stone. He quickly grabbed the hook with both hands as well, but he was pulled five feet farther in. He was stopped because his feet dug into the soil at a sharp angle. Luckily there was some stone steps buried within the dirt that allowed them to brace against the pull.

"Pull!"

The two managed to slowly wrestle the hook out, despite its burning their hands. The pull was like drawing back a two-hundred-pound bow string. Taking it out was just as painful to Don as when it went in.

"Don't let it go!" shouted Amanda.

Don thought she had really lost her mind but went with it, as the last bloody tip of the hook was retracted. The monster made a slight groan within its revolving jaws, as if it too was tired of this tug-of-war. Amanda and Don wrestled the hook back onto the breached crevasse of another support beam. The burning in their arms was relieved tremendously, as the full force of the pressure was now on the frail stone.

To their amazement, the hook ripped out the one slab

and allowed the others to come toppling down. The two had to retreat back up the tunnel quickly, just as the rock and dirt started caving in. Instead of flesh and bones, the beast was overwhelmed by massive boulders, rock, and earth. The first five hundred pounds of it were gobbled, but as more of the tunnel gave way, the grinding ceased, and the mouth was clogged with mostly rock. The grinder was silenced.

The torches were lost in the confusion, and the two were in total darkness, but the relief was enormous as they separated themselves from the terrors within. They couldn't speak while their panting ran its course. Don felt as if he had maxed out double at the gym. Finally, as Amanda caught her breath, she reached for Don. Her hands pulsed with pain.

"You all right? How's the leg?" she asked.

"It feels like shit."

"Can you walk?"

Don grunted but threw an arm over Amanda's shoulders and used the strength in his one leg to get up.

"Well … there's only one way, and that's up. Let's hope this doesn't fork out," said Amanda. There was a long period of hobbling and walking in the dark. The tunnel bent and narrowed but kept leading on. Amanda talked more of her personal life to try to keep Don awake. He became heavy when his strength waned, but Amanda gave him a good nudge and reassurance.

13

Don daydreamed about his family embracing him when he walked through the door, but the thought seemed superficial, as it was most likely he would bleed out from his leg if they did not get help soon. Battered and bloody, the two trudged up until there was a bit of light piercing inward.

Amanda was elated with joy. "Don! Look!"

Don was just as happy, but his injury reminded him to stay put as he tried to help. Amanda could not believe it as she started clawing away at the dirt and rock. The tunnel was at an end, but the end was near the surface. Amanda tore out a stiff root and used that to dig away the loose soil. Her fingers screamed with pain from her burns, but she pried out the large rocks. Her morale was up, and adrenaline kicked in once more as sunlight flooded in.

"What about the wolves?" asked Don, resting off to the side.

Amanda had not even thought about it, but she was ready to take them on, if need be. She had just faced off with creatures not of this world, so wolves seemed like a mere nuisance. She didn't reply, as she heard another voice. Don heard it too. There were distinctive shouts and men barking orders from outside the hole. Amanda laughed and cried all at once as an arm reached in through the hole.

"Hey! Hey, are you all right? Hey, we got someone over here!"

"Hurry!" Amanda called. "We're both hurt. Get us out of here!"

The rescue team above used their tools to clear away a large gap. The day was brighter outside, and the yellow reflective jackets of the firefighters was the greatest sight Amanda had seen. She helped Don limp up to the hole first.

"He needs medical aid. Quick!"

"Okay, get him over here," one said.

They then pulled up Amanda, and instantly the second paramedic tended to her. She noticed that the surrounding woods were crawling with authorities. Plumes of gray smoke clouded the outside of the castle walls. The police had used tear gas to drive off the wolves. The castle was farther away than Amanda had thought. The tunnel led far away from it, and for that she was thankful.

"Jesus, you took one hell of a beating," said the paramedic to Don, who was placed on the stretcher. The paramedic looked at the second-degree burns on Amanda's hands. She was not worried at all, but the sound of rock shifting startled her. The service men also noticed it and looked at the castle, which was mysteriously crashing down. The way the walls folded in along with the castle body indicated that the ground itself must have softened, which weakened the foundation. Amanda could hear the awe in the remarks of the responders, but she knew it was him. Lamonthe was burying his past.

What sort of spirit could topple a structure? The thought vexed her, but in the end she knew the castle was his, and he could take it down just as easily as he'd erected it.

Amanda made her way past the running police and firemen to check on Don, lying on the stretcher. The paramedic was setting up the IV.

"Your one tough college girl. You should consider security or police work," said Don. She smiled and considered the possibility. Her studies had done nothing but lead her to her own ruin, a path that had her dabbling with all the dark parts of history.

"It's okay. I think I'll stick with what I do." She turned and stole one last glance at Black Sun in a heaping ruin. The region officials scratched their heads in confusion as to why it would collapse. Amanda grinned with delight at the sight of it and turned back to Don. "I'll just stay away from castles."

Don managed a smile in return as they loaded him on the ambulance. As they led Amanda toward another ambulance, a camera crew and reporter approached. They shouted and bombarded her with questions in French. A translator was there to relay the questions.

"Miss Cohen! Do you know what happened inside the castle? Are you aware of the dead security guards found just outside?" The bombardment went on from the vultures who sought answers.

Amanda wished she had the right ones. She knew she had to tell them the logical explanation—that she'd been kidnapped and held hostage to help robbers locate treasure in an unknown location. It was going to be difficult to locate whatever was left of Paul's crew, but Amanda knew forensics would play its part. The bullets from the rifles that were fired would surely lead to some black-market transaction, and the surveillance car parked on the side of the highway would be the piece the detectives needed. Maybe the police would even find out if there were more tomb raiders operating in other countries. What did catch her attention was that one reporter talking into the camera was Mark Timbaugh.

What did he have to do with this? None of that mattered now. She was going home to try to forget the nightmare. The trauma would be a scar forever on her conscience.

The reporter was a brunette American woman in jeans and a brown sweater. She made gestures to the castle and stood next to Mark Timbaugh himself.

"From what we can see here, there is nothing much left of the mysterious Black Sun Castle," the reporter said. "Three security guards were found dead. Police have concluded that an intense firefight broke out between them and armed assailants. LPS security Don Millar and analyst Amanda Cohen were safely recovered from whatever disaster befell this once amazing structure. Here I have LPS founder, Mark Timbaugh. Mark, do you have any clue as to what might have happened here?"

The British director leaned over to speak in the mic. "Unfortunately, there is not much I can go off of until police make an accurate report. There will be no questions to my staff until they have recovered, but I do know Phil Orrelle has vanished without any message as to where he might have gone. It's going to be one long investigation."

The trees bobbed around in the steady wind as Amanda stared out the back window of the ambulance that made its way down the highway. She could not help but repeat Lamonthe's words in her head.

"The children of Satan have no boundaries. Soon they will spread throughout the land and consume all that there is."

The pile of rubble that was the castle faded from view. The service crews ran back and forth, prying at the rocks and searching for any other bodies. Away from the search party in the middle of the wreck, something shifted. It was all silent within the windy dust cloud until an unsuspecting black claw-hand reached up from the surface, the talons scratching into the stone. Hell had punched a hole through its limits.

Printed in the United States
By Bookmasters